Second Chances at Mamma's Trattoria

A secret-babies, enemies-to-lovers, second-chance romance set in Italy at Christmas

Stefania Hartley

The Sicilian Mama

ISBN 978-1-914606-50-2
Publisher: The Sicilian Mama

Edited by Sandy Salisbury
Cover by Joseph Witchall

Contents

Chapter 1

Eleonora

Eleonora wiped her tears on her sleeve. They were caused by the onions she had chopped for Mamma's signature pizza sauce, but a moment earlier they had been real tears. Because last night her favourite person in the whole world, Mamma Cristina, had been taken ill to hospital, and Eleonora still hadn't had any news.

A loud yowl made her jump. It was only the cats fighting in the back. She took three calming breaths. She had been on edge since last night, and not just for Mamma's health.

The problem was that her beloved Italian mama had a son, Davide, and he was the last person Eleonora wanted to see again.

Now that his mamma was unwell, he might just abandon the yacht where he was working as a chef and fly back to Calabria. Because blood was thicker than the sparkling waters of the Pacific Ocean.

And thicker than her tomato sauce, by the looks

of it.

Eleonora stirred the watery red liquid in the cooking pot and dropped in a few more chopped tomatoes. She had often helped make *Mamma's* famous sauce but Mamma Cristina had always been in the background giving advice and feedback. This time, instead, Eleonora was flying solo.

She reminded herself that she had trained in the best culinary schools in Italy and bravely dropped in the rest of the tomatoes.

"Mummy, how is Mamma Cristina?" Violetta, the eldest-by-six-minutes of her five-year-old twins, peeked her head through the swinging doors that connected the kitchen to the dining area.

"I don't know, sweetie. We'll find out when the others come back from the hospital."

Eleonora would have liked to visit Mamma Cristina but she wasn't sure if children were allowed in the hospital. Besides, someone needed to stay back at the restaurant and get everything ready to open at seven. Mamma Cristina wouldn't like it if, because of her, they didn't open the restaurant that evening.

A horrible thought came into her head. Perhaps Mamma Cristina would never find out. What if she never came back? *Please, don't take her away*, Eleonora prayed silently.

Mamma was their only family, even if she herself didn't know it. Eleonora would have loved to tell her, but it wouldn't be fair to tell her something she would have to keep a secret from her son.

"But they've been gone ages!" Veronica moaned, peeking her head through the door next to her sister. As they weren't allowed in the kitchen, the girls always kept their toes behind the threshold but leaned in with the rest of their bodies.

"I'm sure they'll be here any moment. Why don't you draw a get-well-card for Mamma Cristina?"

"Okay," the girls said excitedly, and disappeared into the dining room.

Eleonora left the sauce on the hob for a moment and popped out to the garden at the back to pick a sprig of rosemary and a bay leaf, as there was no basil in winter.

The smell of the herbs brought her back to Mamma Cristina. When Eleonora hugged her, she always smelled of rosemary in winter and basil in summer. A wave of nostalgia swept over Eleonora. What if Mamma Cristina didn't come back?

Eleonora chased the thought away and strode back to the stove where the red sauce bubbled like Etna's lava. Right now, all she could do for her most loved woman in the world was to do justice to her tomato sauce.

Chapter 2

Davide

Relief flooded Davide as he pulled out of the hospital's car park and took the road to Altavicia.

He would have rather taken his mamma with him than leave her back in the hospital but, at least, she was on the mend now. Whatever had gone wrong with her heart, the doctors seemed to have fixed it and had reassured him that she should be able to go home soon—on her own two feet, not in a coffin. To say this news had been a relief would be an understatement.

He had got such a scare when he'd got that phone call from the hospital. Luckily, at that time their yacht had been anchored near a city with an airport and he'd been able to jump straight onto a plane. He had taken no luggage, just regrets.

Regret for not calling home often enough. For taking a job that kept him away from home for so long.

Applying to be a chef on a luxury yacht had been a knee-jerk reaction to his divorce. At sea, he had found the peace and the solace he had been looking for. But he had been an absent son.

Anyway, that job was gone now. There was no way his employer could give him all the time off he needed to look after his mamma and her trattoria until she was fully recovered.

His phone rang and, uncannily, the number of Capitano Armorio, the yacht's skipper, came up on the dashboard of the rental car. This call was too important to be taken while driving, so he pulled over.

"Hello, Capitano."

"Hello, Davide. How are you? How is your mum?"

"She seems to be out of danger now."

"I'm glad to hear. You must be relieved."

"I am, but I fear that it will take a while for her to recover fully." This was the moment to broach the difficult subject of his return to work. Davide swallowed. "I'll need to stay here and look after her and the restaurant until she's back on her feet, especially as the Christmas season is always busy..."

He let the sentence hang, waiting for Capitano Armorio to give his verdict. He didn't reply immediately. He must be searching for the right words to let him down gently.

"I don't expect you to keep the job for me. I'll totally understand if you can't wait for me to come back," he said, trying to make it easier for the other man to let him go.

But there was still no answer at the other end.

"Hello?" Davide asked.

The call had been cut off. The yacht often went through patches of poor reception. Davide tried to ring back but he had no luck. Now he had no idea if —assuming he was able to return to the yacht after Christmas—he would still have a job.

This was the problem with being far out at sea: connection was poor. He should be thankful that, at least, the hospital's call about his mum's sudden illness had got through to him. He straightened his back, started the car again and headed for his hometown.

Trattoria Da Mamma Cristina was on the main road leading to Altavicia, just outside the small town, up on a hill that gave it a wonderful view of the sea. It was a rustic building with traditional stone walls and a terracotta-tiled roof which tourists found charming. Davide loved it just because it was home.

But as he drove up the untarmacked lane, he immediately noticed changes. Solar panels on the roof. Mamma hadn't told him anything about them.

Ground lighting signposted the entrance to the car park, which had been extended and marked with potted lemon plants. A big sign hung over the entrance and an old wooden cart full of wheat sheaves was parked decoratively by the door.

The trattoria had had a facelift and he hadn't been told anything about it. Had Mamma made other, bigger, changes without telling him?

Maybe she had hired new staff. Was this why she had made him promise not to fire any staff when he had visited her at the hospital, just now? If this was the case, hopefully it was someone worth keeping on.

Davide got out of the car, walked up the steps to the terrace and walked in through the patio doors. A delicious smell of tomato and rosemary filled the place and, for a moment, he imagined Mamma at the hobs. But, of course, it couldn't be her. Had Mamma employed a cook?

The smell was the same as that of Mamma's signature tomato sauce, but little things inside the restaurant had changed: the gingham tablecloths had been replaced with heavier, dark green fabric. Instead of the white plastic chairs, there were now rustic wooden chairs with straw seats. Cork-stoppered bottles of olive oil sat proudly on the shelves in colour gradation from thick dark green extra-virgin to transparent gold olive oil.

While keeping its rustic look, *Trattoria Da Mamma Cristina* had gone upmarket and he wasn't sure he liked it. Hopefully Mamma hadn't changed many staff: he could do with the comfort of familiar faces.

Chapter 3

Eleonora

From the kitchen, Eleonora heard steps in the restaurant.

"We open at six," she shouted through the door.

Why didn't people read signs?

No apology came from the restaurant and the sound of the steps was getting closer.

She wiped her hands on her apron, marched to the swinging doors and hip-butted them open, ready to give the intruder a polite scolding.

"We're clos—"

The word snagged in her throat.

The moment she had dreaded had arrived. Even with the light behind him, she could recognise his shape in a million. Time at sea had broadened his shoulders and tanned his skin, and he had shaved his head, but it was definitely him. Davide. Her ex-husband.

As her eyes adjusted to the light, she saw the

moment he recognised her too.

His gaze narrowed, frown lines creased his forehead and his stubbly jaw tensed up. Unsurprisingly, it wasn't a friendly look.

When she had decided that her toddlers needed a grandma and she had applied for the job at his mum's trattoria, Davide had just left for a three-year round-the-world sailing trip as a chef on a luxury yacht. Three years had seemed to Eleonora like a very long time, and she had planned to be somewhere else when it was up. But she hadn't planned for emergencies. Like this.

"Hello," she said, trying to sound affable.

He didn't answer back. He just stood there, rigid and motionless, as if he couldn't quite make sense of the sight in front of him.

"How is"—she was about to say "Mamma Cristina" but she thought better of sounding chummy with his mum—"your mother?"

"What are you doing here?" he rasped.

"I work here."

"You must be joking."

"I'm not. I've legally got a job here."

Confusion marbled his face. "How?"

"I applied for it."

"Why would you do such a thing?"

"I needed a job and this one came with accommodation."

Accommodation had been an important factor, but certainly not the main one. Still, this wasn't the time for subtleties and detailed explanations.

That time might never come.

"Now, if you're not going to give me news about your mother, I have jobs to get on with," she said, and made to turn around but he grabbed her arm.

"You can't expect me to believe that you just happen to work for my mother by chance. I'm not that stupid."

"Stupidity is one of the few things I've never accused you of."

"You knew that she was my mother."

"Yes, I did, and I applied for this job because I wanted to work for her. From what you'd told me about her, I guessed she'd be a nice person to work for. This part of the plan was intentional. The part where you return before your job contract on the yacht is up, that part wasn't in the plan."

His eye widened. "You're blaming me for the fact that we're meeting again—when it's you who have wormed your way into my family?"

"No, I'm not."

"Does my mother even know who you are?"

"Of course not. You took great pains to keep me a secret while I was your wife, so I didn't see the point in revealing myself now that we're no one to each other."

In truth, Eleonora hadn't told Mamma Cristina because the sweet old woman would struggle to keep the secret from her son, and it wouldn't be fair to ask her to.

His jaw contracted.

"You've still got a chip on your shoulder about

that."

The chip was more like a boulder. She could understand that they needed to marry in secret because his mother disapproved, but for those few months when they were husband and wife and it was too late for Mamma Cristina to stop the wedding, he could have let her meet his mother.

"What game are you playing, Eleonora?"

"I'm not playing any game. I needed a job and a home, your mother was recruiting and the job came with accommodation, so I applied and got it. If you want to fire me, go ahead. But please, spare us the arguments."

"Quite: we've had enough of those to last us a lifetime," he said bitterly. "Wait. It was you who asked my mother to make me promise..., wasn't it?" he asked, pointing his finger.

"Promise what?"

He narrowed his eyes.

"Don't pretend you don't know."

Many things had infuriated her during their short marriage, but him doubting her honesty had been the worst. "I'm not going to waste any more of my time trying to persuade you that I'm not lying. Could you please answer my original question so I can return to the kitchen where I've got something on the hob? How is your mother?"

At this moment, she felt like she was the one on the hob—boiling, roiling, bubbling and spitting. They had only been in the same room for a few seconds and she already felt her adrenaline surge.

If Davide was going to spend more than twenty-four hours there, she had better keep away from him if she didn't want to lose her sanity.

"My mum seems to be out of danger."

Eleonora let out a breath of relief. This was the first piece of good news of the day.

"But she'll need to rest and take it easy," he continued, "and I'm taking over the trattoria until she's completely recovered, and definitely until Christmas."

Eleonora's heart sank. This was way longer than the twenty-four-hours visit she had braced herself for.

"But what about your job?" she asked hopefully.

"That's none of your concern," he said.

"Fair enough. Then, I'd better go and pack my bags."

She had no idea where she would go. Altavicia wasn't her hometown and, since her parents had split up, moved abroad and got new partners, they had made it clear that their homes were not open to her other than for rare and cursory visits.

It was going to break her and her daughters' hearts to say goodbye to the town they'd grown to call home and the people they considered family. But there was no way she and Davide could work together.

"Why do you taunt me if you know very well that I can't let you go?" he asked.

"Pardon?"

"Don't make me repeat what you already know."

That mistrust again.

"If I had any idea what you're talking about, I wouldn't have asked."

"Or maybe you've asked because you've always enjoyed seeing me beg. Please, stay until Mamma Cristina is back on her feet."

"I'm sure you can manage without me."

"I need you to stay," he said through gritted teeth. "Just till the end of the Christmas holidays."

So Mamma Cristina wasn't coming back in a matter of a few days. Up until yesterday, the sweet woman had been tottering among the tables, taking orders, offering suggestions, dispensing warm smiles. The kitchen still echoed of her gravelly singing voice as she smacked, slapped and stretched the pizza dough.

"What do you want to make you stay? Do you want a salary increase?"

He must have interpreted her silence as a bargaining tool.

"I would never take advantage of your mother like this!" Or of him. Despite their grudges, she wouldn't hit him when he was down. "Of course I don't want a salary increase."

In truth, she was in no position to bargain at all. She was the one without options: if she walked out now, she and the twins wouldn't have a roof over their heads tonight.

But Eleonora would do anything for Mamma Cristina, and if that meant staying and working with her worst enemy, she would do it without batting an eyelid.

"If your mother needs me, I'll stay."

Chapter 4

Davide

Davide closed the door of the office and sank into the chair. He needed to be alone to centre himself and process what was happening.

When he and Eleonora had divorced, he had been convinced he would never see her again. She would go back to Milan, he would travel the world and they'd have no reason to meet again. Fortunately, they had no children tying them together.

Which was a textbook example for "be careful what you wish for", because he had wanted children so much that their marriage had collapsed when she had refused.

Back when they'd got married, she had told him that she didn't want children at that moment but she might do in the future. He had stupidly thought he could wait (or persuade her). But as soon as they got married, she changed her mind:

children weren't going to be on the cards then or ever.

He had felt betrayed and had stopped trusting her. She had accused him of oppressing her, of trying to curb her freedom and of being a stereotypical Southern Italian husband. The last thing he would have imagined was to find her here, in Southern Italy, in the heart of his stereotypical Southern Italian home.

What was she really doing in his mother's trattoria? He didn't buy her explanation for a second. She had trained at one of the best culinary schools in Italy—which was how they had met. She could have got a much better job than at his mother's trattoria.

Did Mamma know who Eleonora was? Was she the reason his mother had asked him not to fire any staff?

Eleonora must have manipulated her, ingratiating her favours for herself. If Mamma had no idea who Eleonora was, she would have welcomed her with her usual warmth and love and Eleonora could have freely abused her trust. But why?

He and Eleonora had hurt each other in equal measures and they had fully agreed on the divorce. He couldn't imagine Eleonora having any reasons for wanting to hurt his mother.

He ran his hands over his face. He already missed the feel of the wind and the sea spray on his cheeks.

He pulled the latest accounts book out of a shelf to see how the business was doing. Mamma had always resisted digitisation and insisted on keeping the books herself, even if she didn't have time.

He opened the latest accounts book and immediately recognised the handwriting, but it wasn't Mamma's. It was Eleonora's.

The fact that he couldn't imagine why his ex-wife would want to hurt his mother didn't mean that she wouldn't. If Mamma had given her access to the admin side of her business as well as the kitchen, Eleonora could have done unimaginable damage to the trattoria.

Had the trattoria's makeover been Eleonora's idea to push Mamma into extravagant spending and ruin her?

He studied the ledger's entries carefully. As he had suspected, there had been considerable expenses. If only he hadn't promised Mamma he wouldn't fire anyone!

Perhaps firing Eleonora wouldn't be the best move after all. Keep your friends close and your enemies closer, as they say. It was going to be extremely unpleasant but keeping Eleonora in the trattoria, where he could keep an eye on her and find out what she'd been up to, might be the wisest choice. After he'd found out exactly what she'd done, he could send her away and repair the damage.

"Who are you?" A child's voice interrupted his

thoughts.

He turned to the door. Two identical little girls he had never seen before seemed extremely preoccupied with keeping their feet just the other side of the threshold.

"I'm Davide, and who are you?"

"Hello Davide. I'm Violetta and she's my twin, Veronica."

Whose children were they? He used to know everyone in Altavicia, let alone in his mamma's trattoria, but these two were strangers.

"Are you allowed to sit on Mamma Cristina's chair?" they asked.

"Yes."

"Why?"

"Because she's my mum."

"He's Mamma Cristina's boy!" the girls said to each other excitedly.

"Mamma Cristina always talks about you," Violetta said. "We've got a mummy, too. Do you know her? She's called Eleonora."

Davide's blood slowed down. It couldn't be the same Eleonora. She hadn't wanted children. There must be someone else with that name.

"She's in the kitchen. She's making Mamma Cristina's tomato sauce," Violetta added.

Could there be another Eleonora in the kitchen, cooking Mamma's tomato sauce? He wanted to believe that it was possible. But as he stared at the little girls, he could see his ex-wife's eyes, her curly hair, even her dimples. These girls looked unmistakably like the Eleonora he had been married to.

It was a good thing that he was sitting down.

Maybe Eleonora had wanted children, just not with him. Who was the father? When had this happened? He wanted to ask the twins how old they were but it felt sly and unfair. He would not use children to spy on his ex.

What he could tell just by looking was that the girls didn't look very young, so Eleonora couldn't have waited very long after their divorce to find another man.

A horrible thought came into his mind. Had Eleonora had an affair before their break-up? The thought made his stomach churn.

He had thought that she couldn't hurt him anymore but there he was, hurting again.

"Girls, where are you?" Eleonora called from the kitchen.

"Goodbye, Mamma Cristina's boy," the girls said in unison and left politely closing the door behind them.

Davide stood up and paced the small room that now felt like a cage. He longed to be back at sea with the albatrosses and the pelicans, among the vast expanses of water, under starry skies, and away from Eleonora.

When he could leave again, it wouldn't be a moment too soon.

Chapter 5

Eleonora

"**. . .** Then roll it in some flour,
and come back in one hour,"
Eleonora sing-songed to herself as she put the pizza dough in the warm oven to rise.

Years of culinary training didn't stop her being nervous about attempting to replicate Mamma Cristina's cooking. The woman had a magical touch.

So Eleonora had made up songs and rhymes to memorise Mamma's recipes and advice. Now that Mamma wasn't around to dispense her suggestions, they were coming in handy.

Time to start the caponata. This was arguably the most hazardous dish on the menu because customers' expectations varied widely. There were thirty-seven different versions of this Sicilian recipe in Sicily alone, and probably even more in Calabria, with each family having their own. It was a highly controversial recipe, and one that was bound to leave some customers disappointed, but it was on the menu and Eleonora had bought the aubergines and all the other ingredients the day before so she had no choice but go through with it on her own.

"Hello, Mummy!" Violetta and Veronica said from the door.

Eleonora smiled to herself. No, she wasn't on her own. Her daughters were still too young to help her make the caponata but they could certainly provide company and good cheer.

"Hello, *tesori miei*, my treasures."

"Have you met Mamma Cristina's boy?" Violetta said.

Okay, maybe not good cheer, if this was going to be their topic of conversation.

"I have. But he's not a boy."

He had been when they met at culinary school and recklessly married, but now he was all man.

"But Mamma Cristina calls him 'my boy'," Veronica said.

"Because, for a mother, her children are always her babies." Eleonora busied herself cutting the aubergines.

"He doesn't look like Mamma Cristina's baby. He doesn't look at all like her," Violetta said.

Eleonora would rather not have a discussion about Davide's looks. She dropped the aubergines into a bowl of salty water.

"Children don't always look like their mum."

She headed for the pantry to fetch the other ingredients.

"...capers, celery and tomato paste
to give your caponata that special taste."

The girls followed her.

"But we look like you."

They were right. They looked a lot more like her than they looked like Davide. A small mercy, Eleonora thought. But she didn't want to go down that line of conversation. So far, she had managed to answer all the girls' questions about their daddy without having to lie just by being vague. But how long would she be able to do that?

"Can one of you find me some sugar?" she asked, for a diversion.

"Yes!"

The girls ran into the restaurant and Eleonora measured the vinegar.

"How many cups, one or two?
Smell the bottle: one might do."

Mamma Cristina always adapted her recipes to the ingredients of that day. This meant that there was no fixed recipe, and attempting to repeat her dishes was like attempting to copy the music of a jazz player.

Why weren't the girls coming back? There were plenty of sugar pots on the dresser. Eleonora marched towards the swing doors and stopped. The girls were talking to someone.

"Mummy says you're not a boy," came Violetta's voice.

Oh, no. They were talking to Davide again.

"What does she say I am?" Davide replied with a hint of curiosity in his voice.

"A baby," Violetta answered.

"Mamma Cristina's baby," Veronica said.

"Interesting."

"But she also said you're a man. Are you a daddy, then?" Violetta said.

Eleonora cringed. This was such a dangerous topic.

"No, I'm not." Davide's voice came as a low rumble.

"Our mummy is a mummy," Veronica said.

"I know that," he said dryly.

It was time to stop this conversation, for everyone's sake. Eleonora burst through the swing doors.

"Girls, where's my sugar?"

Her gaze fell on Davide and her brain whispered that the sugar was right in front of her. With his suntan and his rugged looks, those eyes the colour of the sea in the sun, he was cane sugar, sea salt and caramel all rolled into one.

Yesterday, when she'd seen him again for the first time after all those years, she had been too worried about Mamma Cristina's health to notice that the years, the winds and the oceans had roughened the edges of the boy and turned him into an even more attractive man. But there was no denying that looking at him still gave her the butterflies. And when he looked back, her knees melted a little.

"It's here!" the twins shouted in unison, lifting a sugar pot up into the air so enthusiastically that golden crystals spilled onto the pristine maiolica tiles.

Davide glanced at the floor.

Mamma Cristina had welcomed them into the trattoria as a family package. She had said that her son had grown up pushing his toy cars on the restaurant's tables and the twins were welcome to do the same. But Davide might not be so welcoming.

"Sorry, Mummy. We'll clean it up," the girls said, bending down and spilling more sugar.

"No. Please, put the pot down and go and play upstairs."

Looking crestfallen, the girls obeyed and Eleonora rushed to the kitchen to grab a wet cloth. When she returned, Davide had already cleaned up with a wet paper napkin.

"I'm sorry."

"Why are you cooking?" he asked. "We're not opening tonight."

"Why not? This is what Mamma Cristina would want, I'm sure."

She saw him wince when she said "Mamma" and regretted saying it.

"I'm sure she wouldn't," he retorted.

"Have you asked her?"

"The doctors said that she mustn't be troubled," he said sternly.

"Then all the more reason to open tonight and carry on as normal."

"Do I need to remind you that I'm in charge here now?"

"Your mother is going to hate it when she discovers that we've closed the trattoria because she was unwell. She once told me that she's never closed the trattoria, not even when your father died."

He flinched and she regretted mentioning his father.

"I wonder how many other things she's told you," he spat.

Earlier, when she had agreed to stay, she had imagined Davide sitting in the office, minding the business side of things and keeping out of her hair. But if he was going to interfere in the kitchen it would be too much. Didn't they say, "too many cooks spoil the broth"?

"If this is the way it's going to be, I'm leaving."

"Hello?" someone called from the door. "Eleonora?"

She shot Davide a look that said, "I'm not done with you", and answered as sweetly as she could, "On my way."

Chapter 6

Davide

"D avide!" Paolo said, coming towards him.

Even if it was great to see Paolo again , this wasn't good timing for a childhood friends' reunion.

Paolo had been his best friend all through his childhood and teenagerhood. They had grown up together riding their bicycles first, then their Vespas, up and down the streets of Altavicia, until life had separated them.

Davide had left to go to culinary school, then to live with Eleonora and, last, to go to sea. Paolo had moved to London to study art when his fiancée had left him for his brother. Paolo had been through his own share of heartbreak.

They pulled each other into a bear hug.

"It's so nice to see you! I didn't know you were back in town," Paolo said.

"I rushed back because Mamma was taken into

hospital. But she's out of danger now, and she's recovering well."

"I'm sorry, I didn't know. Do you need any help?"

"I'm fine, thanks."

"You've got Eleonora to help you," Paolo said, smiling at her.

Davide felt a jolt of pain. His best friend knew her too. She had inserted herself into his life completely, while he had absolutely no idea. During the short time they had been married, she had never met his family and friends. And now that they were supposed to have parted ways forever, she had rooted herself into his home and his community.

"Yes, I'm sure she will be a great help," he said, trying to keep the sarcasm out of his voice.

But Paolo knew him well enough to detect that something was off.

"Did you two already know each other?"

"No!" Davide and Eleonora answered in unison.

Paolo smiled.

"Then you have so much to catch up on, mate. Let me introduce to you my fiancée, Alice."

The young woman next to Paolo stepped forward and offered her hand with a smile. Davide shook it warmly. She seemed like a nice girl and Davide was pleased for his friend. After all he had been through Paolo deserved a happy ending.

"Are you here for dinner?" Eleonora asked the couple.

Davide bristled at the fact that she was playing

host.

"We won't be opening tonight," Davide quickly put in before Eleonora promised anything. "Can I offer you a drink instead?"

"No, thank you, but we'd like a word."

"Of course. Take a seat."

Davide pulled out three seats from the nearest table —one for him, one for Paolo and one for Alice —making a point that Eleonora wasn't invited to this reunion.

Eleonora got the message and turned towards the kitchen. But Paolo stopped her.

"Please, stay. We need your help too," he told her. Then he turned to Davide.

"I'm sorry to come knocking on your door when you've got plenty on your plate with Mamma Cristina out of action, but you're the only ones we can trust."

"Ones", plural. Paolo trusted Eleonora as much as he trusted Davide, his best friend from childhood. This must be a joke.

"Paolo and I are getting married. But there is a problem," Alice explained in a laboured Italian. Paolo must have met her in London. He and Paolo had so much to catch up on!

"Our wedding was all organised. We only had the invitations to send out—which we had kept until last to avoid leaks," Paolo continued.

So that was why he hadn't known about this wedding. It wasn't that Paolo hadn't invited him.

"Leaking to who?" Davide asked.

"To the press. Alice's father is Luigi Felice."

"The tenor?"

"Yes."

"I see."

Luigi Felice was an international celebrity and Altavicia's homegrown pride. The tenor used to spend his summer holidays there, at his grandma's place, all through his childhood. Although he had never been Altavicia's full-time resident, he had built himself a villa there. Davide didn't remember the tenor having a wife, partner or children, and Alice clearly hadn't grown up in Italy. There must be a story there. He also wondered how Paolo had met Alice, but this would be a conversation for another day.

"Unfortunately, the press has got hold of the news and the paparazzi are already swarming around Luigi's villa," Paolo said.

"We were going to have our wedding there but it's not possible anymore," Alice explained.

"If we want to dodge the paparazzi, we'll have to change the wedding's venue and date," Paolo said.

Davide still couldn't see how he and Eleonora could help.

"Are you asking us to cater for the wedding?"

Even as he said it, it sounded ridiculous. Mamma Cristina's trattoria did ordinary food—the kind one would eat at home. They could never cater for a wedding, let alone that of a celebrity.

Paolo sucked his breath between his teeth and looked at Alice. Clearly, catering wasn't what they had come to ask. Davide regretted his question, making it awkward for the couple.

"I was only joking," he rushed to add.

"Actually, we'd like you to do more than that," Alice said.

"What would you say if we asked you to host our wedding here?" Paolo asked.

Chapter 7

Eleonora

E leonora was gobsmacked. Hosting the celebrity wedding of the year—something that would make national news and be on gossip magazines the world over—in Mamma Cristina's trattoria would be like having a royal coronation in someone's flat.

"You're joking," Davide said.

Alice bit her lip.

"No. We're serious," Paolo said.

"But Mamma's trattoria isn't glamorous enough for a wedding, let alone a celebrity one," Davide continued.

Alice winced at the word "celebrity".

"That's why the paparazzi won't think of it," Paolo said.

"We're not celebrities," Alice clarified. "We're just normal people and we don't want anything special."

"Alice hasn't grown up as a celebrity's child,"

Paolo explained. "She only found out that Luigi Felice was her natural father a few months ago. And you know me: I'm happy with simple things."

"There are other restaurants and trattorias below the paparazzi's radar which could cater for bigger numbers than we can. Why here?" Eleonora asked, forgetting her resolve to stay out of the conversation.

"Your trattoria is out of town, tucked away in the countryside, up on a hill with only one access road. Paparazzi won't be able to approach without being spotted," Paolo said.

"You're making this place sound like a castle, and your wedding like a siege," Davide said.

"Sometimes it feels like it," Paolo said with a sigh.

"But the main reason," Alice said, "is that we trust you."

Eleonora felt Davide stiffen next to her. What was wrong with what Alice had just said? Did he not feel trustworthy? Surely he wouldn't go telling the paparazzi about the wedding. Unless, of course, the untrustworthy one was her!

"We need someone we can trust in two ways," Alice continued. "First of all, not to sell us to the paparazzi, of course. Second, not to let any information slip accidentally."

Paolo shook his head sadly.

"Unfortunately, the paparazzi got the information from Camillo's brother, Natale."

"Isn't he studying fashion design?" Davide

asked.

"Yes, and to help him out, we've given him the job of designing and making Alice's wedding dress and my wedding suit. Unfortunately, he let the information slip with someone who was working with him and that person didn't keep it to himself."

"Please, help us," Alice begged.

Eleonora couldn't help reaching for the other woman's hand across the table and squeezing it.

She remembered her own wedding. She had told herself that having a secret wedding, with no guests, no party and no wedding dress didn't matter, but when they day arrived, she had felt a twinge of sadness.

But it didn't matter now, because that marriage hadn't lasted and she was never going to get married to anyone again. She was done with men.

Alice looked gratefully at her, then turned to Davide imploringly. Paolo was looking at him too. Eleonora kept her gaze on the table, fearing that Davide might say no just to spite her.

"When would the wedding be?" Davide asked.

Paolo and Alice looked at each other.

"The original date was in April but we've thought that if we have the wedding sooner, we'll have a better chance to dodge the paparazzi," Paolo said.

"How soon is sooner?"

"Christmas Day," Alice said.

"That's in three weeks' time!" Davide said.

Eleonora could see the chances of him agreeing to it getting slimmer by the second.

"We hope that the paparazzi might be distracted on that day—maybe at home with their families," Paolo said.

"Will your guests be able to attend on Christmas Day?" Eleonora asked.

"We think so. We're only inviting close family and close friends."

"Mamma Cristina won't be able to help us," Davide said.

"But you've got Eleonora," Alice said.

Eleonora saw Davide almost imperceptibly wince. He clearly cherished the prospect of working with her as much she with him.

"We don't know where else to turn, Davide," Paolo pleaded.

"Fine. We'll do it," Davide said.

Paolo leant over the table and hugged him. "Thank you. I owe you big."

Davide sighed.

"Be warned: if you complain about the food, the service or anything, you're dead meat," he said half-jokingly.

"There'll be no complaints of any sort!"

Relief washed over Eleonora. Alice and Paolo deserved this. Eleonora didn't know them very well, but she'd heard how Paolo had left Altavicia for London when his fiancée had left him for his brother. She'd also heard that Alice had come to Altavicia with Paolo—back then only a friend—to find her birthmother after discovering, after her parents' death, that she'd been adopted.

But her happiness for the couple was clouded by the realisation that she would have to work with Davide on this project. A wedding, of all things. Could there be two people more disillusioned about romantic love? If Alice and Paolo had known the truth about them, they would have never asked.

"We'd better start planning this wedding right now," Davide said, then turned to her and added with a snide smile of triumph, "How wise of us to decide not to open the restaurant tonight."

Chapter 8

Davide

Davide had had no idea that a wedding required so many things. Paolo and Alice had told him that they wanted the bare minimum, but even that seemed a lot to him: photographers, flowers, wedding car…

It made him wonder whether his and Eleonora's wedding had even counted as one. But it didn't matter now: it certainly didn't count now that it had been erased by their divorce.

It had been a long day and he was tired now. He trudged up the stairs to the flat—his and Mamma's home. As his return had been unexpected, she wouldn't have got his room ready so he'd have to find beddings and towels. They should still be in the store cupboard.

But as he trudged up the stairs, he heard children's voices. They must be Eleonora's daughters. Earlier, she had told them to go upstairs. Were they living in the flat too?

This was too much. He couldn't share the flat with Eleonora! He must find a hotel. He turned around to go to his rental car—the only place he could call his own now.

After a thorough online search, he couldn't find anywhere to stay. Altavicia was a seaside town and most of the hotels were shut for the winter. Of the few which were open, he knew the owners. Questions would be asked, like why he wasn't sleeping at his Mamma's home, and gossips would start. For the same reason, he couldn't ask any of his friends like Paolo to put him up.

Then something else occurred to him. If he left the flat to Eleonora, he would be doing her a favour. Unsupervised, she would have free access to all his mother's belongings, when he still hadn't worked out what she was up to.

Everything pointed to one solution: he must stay at the flat.

He glanced up to the windows. The bathroom light was on. They would have to share the bathroom too. He sighed.

At least Paolo's wedding was only three weeks away. By then, Mamma might be back on her feet and he could ask Eleonora to leave.

He decided to wait in the car until the bathroom light went off. Eleonora might be giving a bath to the girls and the last thing Davide wanted was to be catapulted into the intimacy of Eleonora's family life.

He turned on the car radio. It was heartbreak

songs. He changed the station and found some dance music.

While he was dozing with his head on the steering wheel, dance music blaring on, an email pinged on his phone. The display said it was from Capitano Armorio.

Instantly Davide was wide awake. This must be his dismissal. He opened it resignedly.

"I'm sorry our conversation was interrupted earlier due to poor signal on my side. Whenever you're ready to come back, we'll be here for you—whichever port 'here' will be then. Just give me twenty-four hours' notice and I'll organise transport for you. We are all thinking of you and send our best wishes to your mother for a happy and full recovery.

Best wishes,

Capitano Armorio"

Davide let out a long breath. It wasn't bad news after all. His job wasn't gone. It would still be there for him when he finished in Altavicia. And he couldn't wait for that.

The bathroom light went off and he trudged back to the flat. He slipped inside as quietly as possible, and was relieved to find that his own room was unoccupied and just the way he'd left it before going to sea. His heart squeezed as he realised that Mamma had never lost hope that he'd return.

From the spare room—now presumably Eleonora's room—came the sound of a female voice singing a lullaby.

He had never heard Eleonora sing before and he wouldn't have imagined her singing a lullaby to a child in a million years. He shut himself in his room and put headphones on.

Chapter 9

Davide

D avide was very glad when the doctors said that Mamma Cristina could go home. He had picked her up together with all the gifts and flowers she had received—no doubt driving the poor nurses crazy—and was now driving her home.

He stopped the car right in front of the entrance to the flat.

"I'll carry you up the stairs," he said.

"No way. I can manage on my own," she replied with an amused smile.

"You're still convalescent."

"I don't know what that word means and I don't care. I walked down these stairs to get into the ambulance so I can certainly walk up them now that I've been fixed," she protested.

His mother must really be better if she had her combativeness back.

Eleonora must have been watching from the

window because she suddenly appeared with a big smile. Confusingly, she looked genuinely happy to see Mamma Cristina again.

"But all the saints help going down," Davide told his mother, repeating a popular saying.

"And going up, you and Eleonora will help me. My very own couple of saints," Mamma said with a cheeky smile he knew very well.

His stomach sank. Mamma was going to matchmake between him and Eleonora.

"One on one side, one on the other," she ordered, offering one arm to each.

But the stairs were too narrow for three people and Davide and Eleonora had to climb behind her, holding onto her elbows, squashed together.

Mamma seemed to proceed easily without any help but she had clamped their hands between her elbows and her sides so they had no choice but follow her.

Davide hadn't been so close to Eleonora in years. Her scent hadn't changed. Memories flooded back, not all of them good.

When they reached the top of the stairs, Mamma still didn't release their hands. They continued this procession through the flat all the way to her favourite chair, where she finally enthroned herself.

"Don't go away," she said to them as soon as she had released their hands. "Sit down here and tell me all about Paolo's wedding."

Reluctantly, they sat on the sofa and the chair

next to hers. Davide told her about Paolo and Alice's requests.

"They haven't just asked us to cater for the party. They've asked us to organise everything else too," Eleonora said.

"Why?"

"Because they're being watched by paparazzi. If they or their family members go to florists, car rental shops, or photographers, the paparazzi will immediately be onto the trail. But if Davide or I do it, nobody will suspect," Eleonora explained.

"It makes sense. Have you got any experience of weddings?" Mamma asked Eleonora. "Maybe even your own?"

Mamma was trying her best to sound innocent but Davide could easily tell that she was fishing for marital status information.

Eleonora shifted uncomfortably in her chair.

"Mamma, you can't ask personal questions of an employee," Davide intervened.

"Sweetheart, Eleonora is not just an employee. She's like my own daughter."

Davide did his best not to wince at that.

"I ought to get on with the kitchen," Eleonora said, standing up.

"Whatever the father of the twins has done to you, don't let it put you off all men. Not all of them are bad," Mamma Cristina said, looking pointedly to Davide.

Davide felt like the flat was shrinking around him. He had to get out.

Blushing to her hairline, Eleonora nodded and headed downstairs.

Davide gave her ample time before leaving too so that they wouldn't have to navigate the narrow stairs together again.

But Mamma took her chance to whisper to him, when Eleonora had only barely left the room: "She's a jewel. Don't let her slip through your fingers. I don't know what happened with the father of the girls. Unless the guy died, he's an idiot to have let her go."

Davide swallowed.

"I've got to go."

He made to stand up but Mamma held him back with a hand on his knee.

"Your friend Paolo is getting married. Isn't it time you too thought about settling down?"

"Mamma, you're forgetting that Eleonora is not from Altavicia," Davide said icily.

They had had endless rows about him marrying someone from outside town and, in the end, Mamma had threatened to cut him out of the trattoria if he married a non-local girl.

Mamma Cristina lowered her gaze guiltily. Davide remembered that the doctors had told him that Mamma needed rest. He shouldn't have brought up such a contentious topic.

"Sorry, I shouldn't have said that," Davide apologised.

"Eleonora wasn't born in Altavicia but she's an Altavician now."

"I don't think so. I'm convinced she will leave soon."

Eleonora had no right to embed herself in his world. Altavicia was his home.

Mamma narrowed her gaze at him. "Why should she leave? Have you upset her?"

"I haven't done anything."

Not now, at least. And what had happened in the past wasn't just his fault.

"Good. Then continue to be nice to her and she might stay. If you work with her to help your friend get married, maybe Heaven will give you a wedding of your own soon too."

Chapter 10

Eleonora

Eleonora got onto her bicycle and rode away from Paolo's house.

The four of them had agreed that it wasn't safe for Paolo and Alice to visit the trattoria again, in case that raised suspicions either among fellow Altavicians or among paparazzi lurking around. Instead, Eleonora and Davide would meet them at Paolo's home. Davide being Paolo's old-time friend, even frequent visits wouldn't raise suspicions.

Eleonora and Davide had immediately divided all the tasks between them—catering, florist, car rental—so that they could visit the couple separately and wouldn't have to spend more time together than strictly needed.

To Eleonora's surprise, they hadn't spent much time together at all. Despite sharing a flat, a job and a wedding project, they barely saw each other. The restaurant being busy must have helped, but

Eleonora suspected that the main reason was that they both tried to avoid each other. Paradoxically, in this respect, they were truly working together.

Eleonora stopped outside the florist and leaned her bicycle against the wall. Since coming to Altavicia, she had learnt that nobody would steal a bicycle—or anything else. There would be no point because everyone knew what belonged to whom.

Giovanni's shop wasn't just a florist but also a bookshop. Eleonora would have never thought that flowers, which need water, and books, which must be kept away from water, would be good shelf-fellows, but Giovanni made it work so well that "The Scarlet Pimpernel"—that was the name of his shop—didn't feel incongruous.

Giovanni's face lit up when she entered.

"It's lovely Eleonora! Must be my lucky day. What can I do for you? Will it be books, flowers or both today?"

"Only flowers, please," Eleonora said.

"I have some lovely camelias for you and some pansies for the girls," Giovanni said, already looking around the shop.

"They're not for us and they're not for now. I need to order some flowers for Christmas for the trattoria."

"I thought you'd be closed on Christmas Day," Giovanni said.

"We're having a private party."

This was close enough to the truth. Anything more and she would have to be very careful. She had discussed with Paolo and Alice exactly what she was to say if people enquired. Altavicia was a small place and news travelled very quickly, especially anything to do with Luigi Felice or his daughter.

"A private party? How exciting. I guess it's because Mamma Cristina's son is back," Giovanni said, pausing as if he was studying her reaction.

Eleonora froze for a moment. Did Giovanni know? How was that possible?

"It's to celebrate Mamma Cristina's recovery," she said awkwardly.

"I expect Mamma Cristina would love to see you together," Giovanni continued.

"I don't know what you mean," Eleonora said coldly.

She had walked into Giovanni's shop ready to protect Alice and Paolo's secret but now it was her secret that seemed to be in danger.

"I mean that Mamma Cristina would surely like to see her son married to a lovely woman like you. But if you decide to take on a husband, remember that I got to know you before him," Giovanni said with a wink.

Relief washed over her. So this was just jealousy. Giovanni didn't know about her past with Davide. He was just calling dibs on her. She smiled.

"That's very kind, thank you."

Then she told him about the flowers and greeneries she wanted to order—the ones Paolo and Alice had chosen. They were poinsettias, holly, ivy and butcher's broom plus, of course, mistletoe. Alice and Paolo had preferred to stick to typically Christmassy decorations to give their wedding a better chance to go unnoticed by the paparazzi. But there was still one item that could give it away.

"I also need a bouquet."

"What kind of bouquet?"

Eleonora described it, Giovanni made a note of flowers and shape and colour combination.

"Basically, what you want is a wedding bouquet," he said eventually, looking up at her.

She averted her gaze. He must have mistaken that for shyness, because he immediately— and passionately—said, "Oh, Eleonora, if you're looking for a husband, look no further."

"Er… thank you, but I'm not. I just need a nice bouquet for my girls. They've put it on their list for Santa," she lied.

"I see." He sounded disappointed.

He then said that he should make two bouquets, one for each of the twins. Eleonora agreed, even if that was going to cost more. Even though she was sure that Alice and Paolo wouldn't mind paying a little more for the sake of their privacy, Eleonora decided that she would pay for the extra bouquet herself.

She left the shop confident that the flower arrangements were in safe hands and would be done with the utmost care. She was about to straddle her bike and ride back to the trattoria, when she had a feeling that something was off.

Had she forgotten something inside the shop? She peered through the window and Giovanni waved cheerfully at her. No, all was well.

All this cloak-and-dagger business around the wedding must have made her paranoid. She brushed that feeling away and set off.

But when she was taking the turning up the hill towards the trattoria, she noticed that a man on a scooter—riding very slowly—was following her.

Chapter 11

Davide

Davide discovered that he could do a lot of work from the trattoria's tiny office, and all that week he managed to keep mostly to himself.

The suppliers were all booked for what he had passed as a large family Christmas party. The fact that he didn't have a large family and the few relatives he had lived far from Altavicia meant that nobody could deny the party's reality or feel offended at not having been invited.

As far as he could tell, the only danger was Mamma Cristina. She was a sociable and chatty lady and she could accidentally let slip information about the wedding. So long as she was confined to their home to recover—that is, until her next medical check-up, Paolo and Alice's secret should be safe.

Davide finished typing the wedding menu on the office laptop and saved it. An email popped up on the screen. It was from the bank.

Davide opened it. The trattoria's account was in overdraft.

It made no sense. He had checked the trattoria's accounting books and they showed a healthy profit. Where had the money gone?

He logged onto the online banking. The transactions log showed several cash withdrawals. Who had taken that money?

The withdrawals had stopped the day before he arrived. A shiver ran down his spine. Eleonora.

During their brief marriage, she had been shown to be untrustworthy—first saying that she might want children one day, then saying she never would—but he had never imagined her a thief.

There might be a very good explanation for these withdrawals. He must ask Mamma if she knew anything about them. But not yet. First, she needed to recover completely. A drama like missing money and a thief in their home could tip her over the edge again. He would just have to keep his eyes open and investigate the matter on his own.

He looked out of the window. Eleonora was riding up the hill.

He had never seen her on a bicycle or had any idea that she could ride. That just showed how little he had known her before he asked her to marry him. How stupid of him.

A man on a scooter was riding behind her. He

must be following her because no one would ride a scooter so slowly. He could be a stalker, a suitor, the father of the twins or all these things together. Again, this showed how little he knew about her or what she'd been up to in those years they'd been apart.

Davide used his phone's camera to zoom in on the guy. He didn't look like he could be the father of the girls.

Eleonora stopped the bicycle and the man caught up with her. From what Davide could see through the phone's camera, Eleonora's posture was less than friendly and it didn't look like she knew the guy or was pleased to see him. Was he harassing her?

Davide felt like rushing out and confronting the man, but then reminded himself that Eleonora wasn't his wife anymore and she would surely feel offended by his intervention. She could look after herself, he could hear her say, and he should mind his own business.

Stuff what she would say. He couldn't leave her in trouble.

He rushed downstairs, jumped into the car and drove fast down the hill.

Chapter 12

Eleonora

E leonora couldn't believe what the man was saying.

"You've followed me from Paolo Rondino's house to the florist's shop and now almost home because you think I know some secret?" she asked.

She had heard about paparazzi—ironically, from the kind of magazines they worked for—but she hadn't fully realised how intrusive they could be.

"I already know that Luigi Felice's daughter is getting married on 14th April at Luigi Felice's villa. I'll pay you good money for any more information you can give me about it. Are you catering for the wedding? I want to know everything about the wedding's arrangements: the menu, the guests' list, the wedding cake…anything you know. And if, on the day, you can let me into the villa, I'll pay you even more."

"Do you feel that spying on people is an honest

way of making a living? Aren't you ashamed?" she snapped at him.

Just then, a car approached, slowed down and stopped next to them. It was Davide.

Eleonora could have never imagined she'd be so happy to see her ex-husband.

Davide got out of the car and moseyed towards them in a way that looked at once casual and menacing.

"Everything alright here? Had a puncture?"

"This fellow is offering money in exchange for information about a celebrity wedding," she said.

Davide stopped in front of the paparazzo and looked down at him. Eleonora knew that Davide never used violence, but with his shaved head, stubbled jaw and tanned sailor skin, he looked every bit like a man who would punch.

"We don't have any information. And even if we did, we would never give it to you and your kind," Davide said in a low, menacing rumble. "Because this town looks after its own, and Luigi Felice and his family are our own. So skedaddle out of here and don't go around talking to people about a wedding you're not even supposed to know about."

The man shook his head in a gesture that looked halfway between disappointment and disapproval.

"And if you ever come close to my"—Davide hesitated—"colleague again, you'll have the police on your tracks and a criminal record for stalking and harassment."

Eleonora was surprised. She had expected Davide to be protective of Paolo and Alice but not of her. She was nothing to him anymore. In fact, she was worse than nothing: an ex-wife he had clearly shown he'd rather not have met again. Where did this protectiveness come from?

"But if you do change your mind, my offer still stands for both of you, and it'll be more generous than you imagine," the man said, offering his business card.

"Go away," Davide growled without picking up the card.

The man quickly dropped the card back into his shirt pocket, turned his scooter around and zoomed down the hill.

"Be careful. I'm sure he won't leave Altavicia," Davide said, watching him ride away.

Eleonora nodded and continued watching the guy even when it was clear that he wasn't coming back.

It was awkward for her and Davide to be allies rather than enemies, and she didn't know what to say.

"Well, thank you for backing me up," she said.

She knew that she could have handled the man on her own, but it was always nicer to have someone backing you up and fighting your corner. Or was it Alice and Paolo's corner? It didn't matter.

"I was just driving past on an errand. I'd better go."

"Okay. Then, I shall see you later."

He went back to his car and she mounted her bike and headed home.

It wasn't much later that she heard his car returning, and suspected that the errand was just an excuse.

Chapter 13

Davide

Davide turned the spanner on the water pump a bit too hard. He was cross with himself for what had happened earlier.

He shouldn't have rushed to Eleonora's rescue like a knight in shining armour. She was not in danger and she was a strong woman, perfectly capable to tell a paparazzo where to go.

His anger at the paparazzo had only been on Paolo and Alice's behalf of course, Davide told himself. It was simple: he was protective of his best friend. Not of Eleonora.

He stopped tightening the nut and turned on the pump. It sounded much better now.

He rested his back against one of the olive trees and looked down the olive grove stretching all the way to the sea. His home was beautiful even in winter. The trees' evergreen leaves shimmered in the breeze, flashing their silvery sides like an iridescent terrestrial sea.

He had seen blue oceans, green coves, and turquoise bays, but nothing could match the beauty of his own home.

"Hello," a small voice came from behind him.

He didn't need to turn around to know that it was one of the twins. He just didn't know if it was Violetta or Veronica. Probably both, as they seemed to go everywhere together. Davide couldn't fully imagine what it might be like to have such a partisan and loyal companion as a twin seemed to be.

During the day, Davide tried to keep away from Eleonora and the girls, but at night he couldn't escape. He heard them playing in the bath when he and Mamma had their supper—thankfully, Eleonora always declined Mamma's invitations to join them for meals. He heard Eleonora sing them lullabies and then the girls sing each other to sleep. He sometimes heard them squabble over the breakfast biscuits or some lost hairclip, when he waited in his room for them to leave the flat so he could have his breakfast alone.

So, even if he hadn't seen them or interacted with them very much, he felt like he knew the little girls quite well.

"Hello," he said, turning around with a smile.

As he had guessed, the girls were both there.

"What are you doing?" one of them asked.

"I've just finished repairing the water pump."

"But what are you doing now?"

"I'm admiring the view," he answered candidly.

"What are you two doing?"

"We've come to bring you your lunch."

Ah yes, lunch. The sun was going down. It must be well past three o'clock and he felt quite peckish.

"Thank you."

"It wasn't us. It was Mummy's idea."

"But she doesn't want us to tell you that. She told us to tell you that it's from Mamma Cristina," the other girl said.

"Well, that can stay between us," Davide said with a smile, and made a mental note never to entrust any secrets to the girls, should he think of doing that in the future.

They handed him a covered plate and he put it down on a rock.

"Come on, open it," they said, as they stood there instead of leaving.

"Oh, sorry. You need the cover back."

"No, we don't. We just want to see if you like it."

"And we're going to keep you company while you eat."

"That's nice," he said, sitting on a rock.

He wasn't used to eating with an audience, but then he wasn't used to living with children either.

To his surprise, the girls squeezed next to him, one on each side.

Davide lifted the napkin and found a pasta bake. It was a simple, wholesome, homely dish. Nothing that a well-trained chef like Eleonora would use to show off, compete or impress. Her gesture of sending him lunch had no ulterior motives but to feed him.

"Open the napkin and put it on your legs so you don't spoil your clothes if you spill," one of the girls said.

He smiled. Her words sounded just like what a mother would say.

"You're a judicious girl," he praised her.

"What's 'judicious'?"

"Sorry, that's a big word. It means 'sensible', 'wise'."

"Don't be sorry. We like big words."

"Can you teach us more?"

"Okay."

By the time he finished his lunch, the girls had learnt several words to describe the various shades of blue of the sea in front of them, and the colours and texture of the olive trees' bark and leaves.

"I think you should go back now or your Mummy will be worried about you," he said. Not that he hadn't enjoyed their company—far from it.

He had always wanted to have his own children, but he now realised that it was more a desire for a legacy than a yearning for actual little people. He had always imagined his children already grown-up.

"We can stay a little longer," one girl said.

"Mummy won't worry about us. She's always very busy."

"She's always too busy to play with us."

"That's why she's made two of us, so we can play together."

"No. There are two of us because she had been very good and Father Christmas gave her double the presents," her sister contradicted her.

"No, silly. She asked the stork, not Father Christmas," the first girl retorted, piqued.

Davide had no wish to delve into whose help Eleonora had enlisted to have her children.

"In any case, it's good that you can play together," he said conclusively.

"Who did you play with, when you were a boy?"

Davide remembered long days roaming these olive groves on his own, sometimes swimming in the sea with Paolo, and mostly helping Mamma and Papà at the trattoria. When he was a teenager, he discovered that he enjoyed cooking. He had never considered it before because the trattoria's kitchen was his parents' domain and Davide didn't like being told what to do. But when he started imagining he could have his own kitchen, then he realised that he wanted to become a chef.

"I liked playing on my own."

"We like playing together," the girls said. "And with you."

"There you are!" Eleonora's voice came from behind him.

"Sorry," he said, standing up as if he had been caught doing something he shouldn't.

He felt guilty for enjoying the company of these children who didn't belong to him.

But Eleonora didn't look cross. Instead, she smiled.

Her smile, that plate of pasta in his hands, the two girls—one on each side of him, shuffling closer to him as if to guard him or to prevent being taken away—it all felt very homely. As if they were a family. Any passerby who saw them at that moment would be sure that they were a family. For an unsettling moment, Davide felt sure of that too. The girls playing among the same trees, rocks and soil where he had played at their age. A grandma resting upstairs in the flat. A mum and a dad smiling at each other.

Only, he wasn't the girls' dad.

It was such a shame. He and Eleonora could have had all this but she hadn't wanted it.

As he met her gaze, he sensed that she was thinking the same. Why had she rejected his dream of a family, only to make it happen now in this cruel parody-sort-of-way?

"I thought you girls might be troubling Davide. Leave him in peace and come inside."

"Can he read us a book?"

"No," Eleonora replied just at the same time as he said, "Yes."

"But only if your mum says it's okay," he quickly added.

Eleonora hesitated.

Was she reluctant for his sake or the girls' sake? Did she worry that he might be a negative influence on them? Or that they might get attached to him and be sad when he left, after Christmas?

The girls clamoured and Eleonora relented.

"Fine. Go in, wash your hands and choose a book."

While the girls ran towards the house, to Davide's surprise Eleonora hung back.

"I'm sorry about that. Whenever the girls annoy you, please, feel free—"

"Eleonora, please," he interrupted. "I don't mind them. You know that I like children."

He stopped short of adding, "you know how much that I wanted children". The past was too painful a territory and there was no point rehashing it.

"But if it upsets the girls' father—"

"No, no, it's not that."

"Is he still around?" Davide couldn't resist asking, and immediately chastised himself for it.

"It's complicated."

"Of course. These things always are."

"No, not for you. You've had a mum and a dad, and you were a family. Very simple. That's what I've always envied you for. That's why I've chosen to come and work at your mum's trattoria. I wanted the girls to have the same as you've had. But of course, that's not possible."

Davide was surprised at that intimate, sincere sharing. Now he had even more questions than before.

But they had reached the house and the girls were coming towards them with their books and big excited grins.

Chapter 14

Eleonora

It poured with rain. The road that led up to the trattoria had turned into a torrent of mud and the baker's boy refused to deliver that day's bread.

"If I can borrow your car," Eleonora said to Mamma Cristina, "I'll collect the bread from the baker's."

In the past, Mamma Cristina had baked bread herself, and the results had been delicious, but their baker's bread was on another level of deliciousness, so it was worth the trip.

Also, Eleonora was glad for an excuse to be out of the flat. Since Davide's arrival, it had felt too small.

"Of course you can borrow my car," Mamma Cristina replied with her lovely smile. "Leave the girls with me. We'll entertain each other. And thank you for going in this horrible weather."

The baker's narrow street was clogged with cars

parked as close as possible to the shop's entrance to avoid getting their fresh bread wet in the rain. Clearly, the baker hadn't cancelled just the trattoria's delivery.

Eleonora parked on the next street and got soaked on her short dash to the shop. Inside, she met lots of villagers she knew. They greeted each other and exchanged a few words.

Eleonora reflected that it was nice being part of a community like Altavicia. What a pity that, with Davide back, she would have to leave sooner than she had planned.

The baker, Signora Geraci, took back the trattoria's stale bread from Eleonora to turn it into breadcrumbs, and handed her a large parcel with today's bread, wrapped in paper and plastic, to protect it against the rain.

"Sorry we couldn't deliver today," Signora Geraci apologised. "Our van is broken."

"It's okay. I've taken Mamma Cristina's car."

"How is she?" Signora Geraci asked, despite the queue of customers waiting to be served.

"Much better, thank goodness. She's back home now."

"Excellent. And it's a good thing she's got her son back with her. How is he?"

"He's fine."

Eleonora's back automatically stiffened at the mention of Davide.

"He's been away for ages...how long has it been?"

Not long enough, Eleonora thought.

"A while," she said.

"Had you met him before?" Signora Geraci continued.

Eleonora was surprised that there was no impatient clearing of throats from the queueing customers behind her. Instead, she had a feeling that they were interested in listening to their conversation.

"No," Eleonora lied.

If she admitted to having met Davide before, there could be more questions and more complicated lies to invent.

"Is he still single?" the baker asked.

Her matchmaking intentions were so obvious that Eleonora blushed.

"I don't know."

"Well, it's time that man found a wife. Someone his mother would approve of...maybe even someone she already likes?"

Signora Geraci winked and Eleonora felt like the entire shop was winking with her—including the bread buns on the counter. There was no other way to respond but to feign ignorance.

"Must dash. Thank you for the bread. Take care."

"And you—take care of yourself and your daughters. All little girls should have a good dad looking after them," Signora Geraci replied.

Eleonora reached the door not a moment too soon. She ran to the car, as much to escape any more conversation on that topic as to dodge the rain.

She shoved the bread into the boot then dived into the driving seat. And froze.

A man was sitting next to her.

"It's you again!" she exclaimed, recoiling. "You can't just let yourself into other people's cars!"

"And you should lock your car even if you're only stepping out for a moment," the paparazzo said.

"Get out!"

"Not until you've heard me."

"I'm calling the police."

"Why, so you can lie to them too?" the man said with a smirk.

"What are you talking about?"

"You've just told the baker that you had never met Davide before. But I've done some research and I've discovered that you and Davide were married."

Eleonora's blood ran cold.

"That lie was a poor choice. It would be very upsetting for your fellow townsfolk and friends to discover that you and Davide have lied."

Of course he would blackmail her.

"And if you're capable of lying to your friends, you've probably lied to me too when you said you didn't know anything about Luigi Felice's daughter's wedding. But I'll give you another chance to put things right with me. If you tell me everything you know about the wedding, I won't spill your secret."

This wasn't just her secret but Davide's too. If the truth came out, everyone would be upset with him too. Mamma Cristina would be broken-hearted. She would lose her trust in Eleonora and, maybe, in Davide too.

The paparazzo smiled smugly.

"And I suspect that your girls are his too," he said, studying her face.

Eleonora was stunned.

"Excellent. Your reaction has just confirmed that I've guessed right and that, most likely, Davide doesn't know."

"You're not a man. You're a snake," Eleonora hissed.

"Don't worry, Eve. All your secrets are safe with me, if you cooperate."

Eleonora was about to shout that she would never do anything for him, but she stopped herself. Being impulsive with this guy was dangerous. She had already given away her daughters' paternity with her unguarded reaction. She had to play this cool.

One thing working in her favour was time. The man believed that the wedding was on the 14th of April. If she let him believe that this was still the case and fed him other false information, she could buy time.

But he would eventually discover that she had tricked him, so she would have to tell Mamma Cristina and Davide the truth before then.

Chapter 15

Davide

The heavy rains had flooded the trattoria's carpark. Davide went out to investigate the cause and found that the drains were blocked.

Small animals often made nests inside the pipes during the dry summer months so he didn't want to clear them without checking first. He needed a drain inspection camera.

Hoping the hardware shop would be open, he got into his car and headed to town.

The rain was lashing down and the roads were deserted of pedestrians and cars. As he travelled down Altavicia's main road, he noticed Mamma's car parked in a corner, just off the baker's road. Eleonora must have gone to collect the bread.

Something jarred. There were two people in the car, a driver and a passenger—a man.

Davide immediately pulled over.

He knew he shouldn't do this. Eleonora's life

didn't concern him anymore and she had a right to her own privacy. But this was Mamma's car. Did this give him some right to be curious?

He turned off the engine and watched them through his rearview mirror.

Was this man the girls' father? Were he and Eleonora still together? The thought gave Davide an unpleasant feeling in the stomach. If these two were going to part with a kiss, he didn't want to see it.

He was about to turn on the engine again and leave, when he saw them shake hands. This wasn't the way lovers or ex-lovers parted. This looked like a business deal.

Davide stayed and saw the man get out of the car. He was the paparazzo.

This was so much worse than anything he had expected to witness. Eleonora was in cahoots with the enemy! She was a traitor in the bosom of the family.

In the last few days, seeing her take care of his mother with evident affection, Davide had ditched his suspicions about Eleonora. He had come to believe that she was honest and genuine. When she told him that she had come to Altavicia to give her girls the same things that he'd had—a loving family, in the person of Mamma Cristina—he had believed her.

But now it was clear that she must not be trusted.

Before Eleonora could see him, he drove off—

no longer heading to the hardware shop but to the bank.

Davide dived out of the car and into the bank with the urgency of someone going to A&E. He couldn't bear a moment longer without knowing the truth.

The bank manager, Attilio, was a good friend of his. Davide asked for him. Thankfully, he was available.

"What a pleasure to see you!" Attilio said, meeting him in the lobby. "I'm sorry about the reason that has brought you back to Altavicia, but I hear your mum is on the mend, am I right?"

Davide was no longer used to how quickly news travelled in Altavicia and was a little surprised. But it also made sense that a good bank manager should make sure to know all his clients' news and movements so that he could spot any fraudulent use of their accounts.

"Yes, she is, thank you."

"Have you come to say hello or is there anything I can do for you?"

"I hope there is something you can do for me."

"Let's go into my office."

Attilio's office was a windowless room with a bright but cold overhead neon light.

Davide felt sorry for his friend. He would never swap the wide, open oceans for a place like this, no matter how comfortable, secure and well-remunerated.

Attilio must have mistaken Davide's gaze

roaming the room for appreciation, because he said with pride, "I moved office when I was promoted."

"There are no windows," Davide blurted out.

"That's for privacy. It wouldn't be right for passersby to peek in on the bank manager's desk and screen."

That made sense, Davide thought, especially in a small town like Altavicia, where people already knew everything about each other.

Attilio offered him a chair and they both sat down. Attilio rested his elbows on his desk and, steepling his hands, looked at Davide enquiringly.

For a moment, Davide felt like he was in a church's confessional booth—only, the sin he was about to report was someone else's.

"I need your help to find out what's happening to the trattoria's bank account. A lot of cash has been withdrawn from the cashpoint recently, and we're in overdraft."

"Does your mother know anything about it?"

"I don't know and I don't want to ask her. She's convalescent and, if my suspicions are true, she doesn't know anything about it. Then discovering the withdrawals would be upsetting for her—and dangerous, given her health condition."

Attilio frowned.

"So you have some suspicions."

"Yes. Someone my mum has hired after I went to sea. This person is employed as a chef but seems to be doing the trattoria's accounts too."

"Are you talking about Eleonora?" Attilio asked.

Drats. He knew her too. Had his ex-wife infiltrated absolutely every corner of Altavicia—and of his life?

"Yes, that's the one," Davide said with a sigh.

"I would be very surprised if she was doing anything unpleasant, let alone illegal..."

Oh, no. Eleonora had charmed him too.

"You have only just met her, I assume?" Attilio asked.

Davide cringed inside. He hated to lie to his friend and bank manager, but how could he not? Not even his own mother knew the truth about him and Eleonora.

"Yes."

"That explains it. I really wouldn't worry about her. She's a thoroughly good woman, one in a million. The other day, she found a wallet with a bank card and lots of cash just outside the bank. It was someone's pension, which had just been withdrawn. She came in and handed it in to our cashier. Not a cent was missing."

Davide wanted to tell him that they should worry about her, because he'd just seen her shaking hands with a paparazzo to sell Paolo and Alice's privacy to him for money, but he couldn't say that.

"Then could you check the ATM machines' cameras to find out who has been taking the money?" Davide asked.

"I can't do it from the branch. It's something for

the people in the fraud department. Not a simple thing."

Attilio thought for a moment, rapping his fingers on the table.

"I might be able to help you. I have a friend there who owes me a favour. But I won't be able to give you the footage. You'll have to trust me to identify the person. I know everyone in Altavicia, so it won't be hard. I'll certainly be able to tell you if it was your mum or Eleonora or someone else from the trattoria."

"Thank you, Attilio. I owe you."

"I know. Everyone does," he joked.

Chapter 16

Eleonora

E leonora was still rattled by the morning's meeting with the paparazzo.

Pretending to be on his side had been a difficult piece of acting. Shaking his hand had been utterly unpleasant.

Thankfully cooking was always a balm for her, and it was exactly what she needed to do now. She parked the car and headed to the kitchen with all the bread.

The girls were upstairs with Mamma Cristina and would be happy for a while. Davide's car was out. With some luck, Eleonora could unwind on her own in the kitchen as she prepared the breaded cutlets she would be serving for the fixed-menu lunch.

The lunchtime customers were usually a mixture of passing traffic—little, at this time of year—local builders working on the villa up the road, and farm workers. Weekday lunches were a bit like having friends over for lunch. You more or less knew who would turn up, and you served them the fixed menu you had chosen.

Knowing the guests and their preferences, she adapted the fixed menu to their tastes so that nobody was disappointed.

Tano, who always arrived in his bulldozer, liked his cutlet twice breaded, so Eleonora passed his cutlet through flour, egg and breadcrumbs twice.

Mimmo, the sheep farmer, who came only on market days and always gave them some fresh sheep ricotta, he liked deep-fried breaded bread. Today Eleonora would give him a little surprise and hide a slice of mozzarella between two pieces of bread, before coating them in eggs and breadcrumbs and frying them together.

Pippo liked his cutlets paper-thin—barely a support for the breading—so she sliced his cutlet lengthways several times until it was larger than the plate.

The others were happy with anything so long as the wine was good.

She put the prepared cutlets on plates, to be fried only when the guests had arrived, sat down and worked on the sauteed potatoes. Those had to be cooked beforehand.

"Something smells nice," Mamma Cristina's voice came from the bottom of the stairs.

Eleonora jumped.

"How did you get here?"

"On my two feet. I'm not an invalid, darling, and

I feel quite okay today."

"But you haven't had your doctor's checkup yet."

Eleonora quickly wiped her hands, ready to catch Mamma Cristina should she collapse or stumble or, even, float away.

Mamma Cristina smiled.

"I'm fine. Never been stronger. I can feel it in my bones all the strength of the rest I've had in the last few days. All I needed was some rest and seeing my handsome boy."

Eleonora tensed. Every mention of Davide put her on the defensive, ready to protect her secret.

"And if you're worried about your girls, they're watching a Japanese animation about volleyball players. We'll be safe until we turn it off and they start trying to copy the players' moves inside the house," Mamma Cristina said with a chuckle.

Eleonora could easily picture her girls launching cushions across the sofa as if they were volleyballs.

"And you're here just to supervise me—not to lift a finger," Eleonora admonished.

She dragged a chair in from the restaurant and plonked it behind Mamma Cristina, who sat down obediently.

"I've missed being in the kitchen," Mamma said.

"And I've missed you."

Mamma Cristina chuckled.

"I don't know about that. You got Davide instead. A good exchange, if you ask me."

Eleonora stiffened. There it was—another of Mamma's not-so-subtle matchmaking attempts.

Maybe her visit downstairs wasn't motivated by her desire to supervise Eleonora's cooking after all, but to push her matchmaking agenda.

Elenora hated lying to the sweet woman. She had to tell her the truth about her and Davide —certainly before the paparazzo did. But she couldn't spill the beans without obtaining Davide's agreement first. Their past together wasn't just Eleonora's secret but his too.

"What do you think of my son?" Mamma asked.

Eleonora busied herself with the cutlets. Today it wouldn't be just Tano to have his cutlet breaded twice, but all the diners.

"He seems like a nice man."

Mamma Cristina smiled proudly.

"He is. And he loves children."

Eleonora knew that very well. This had been the stumbling block that had brought their marriage crashing down.

"Forgive me for being old-fashioned, but I think that some men might resent bringing up another man's children. Davide wouldn't. I know him and I'm sure that he'd love to be a stepdad to the girls. I've seen them reading books together, and I know him. He would make a great dad."

This conversation was kneading Eleonora's heart like bread dough. Eleonora wished she could run away from it without upsetting Mamma Cristina. The poor woman just had no idea.

"It's my fault that he hasn't got a wife yet," Mamma Cristina said, a cloud sweeping through her face.

Eleonora almost spilled the egg. If Davide's marital status were anyone's responsibility, it had to be hers. If they hadn't divorced each other, he would still be married. And if he was still single years after their divorce, it might be that their turbulent marriage had put him off relationships forever. So Eleonora would have done better to steer away from that topic.

Instead, she felt compelled to ask, "Why should it be your fault?"

Mamma Cristina looked embarrassedly at her lap.

"Years ago, when Davide went away to culinary school, I missed him terribly. My only consolation was that he would be coming back. But then I thought, what if he married someone that wasn't from Altavicia and set up home somewhere else? I was convinced I would die if that happened. So I told him that he could never marry a girl that wasn't from Altavicia."

This matched with what Davide had always told her—why he couldn't introduce her to his family and friends, show her his hometown, have a proper wedding. During the worst times of their marriage, when she lost trust in him, she wondered whether he had just made excuses because he was embarrassed of her for not wanting children. Now she knew that what he had told her was the truth.

"Then he told me he had met a girl at culinary

school and he wanted to marry her," Mamma Cristina continued.

Eleonora froze. That was her. She had always assumed that Davide hadn't told his mum about her.

"I could tell that he was really in love with her and I panicked because she was from Milan. I was sure that she would never want to live in Altavicia and work in our trattoria, with all her exceptional culinary training." Mamma Cristina took a deep breath. "So I told my boy that, if he married her, I would cut him off from the trattoria. I knew that he loved the trattoria, so I thought that, if his love for me wasn't enough to stop him marrying this girl, his love for the trattoria was."

Mamma Cristina sighed.

"Instead, he gave up both me and the trattoria and left. We were both very upset with each other and we lost touch for a while. We eventually reconciled, but then he went to sea. Maybe to run away from me? I wouldn't blame him if he did, because I've been very bad to him."

Tears pricked the back of Eleonora's eyes. Davide had never told her about his mother's ultimatum.

He had given up the trattoria for her and had never told her.

How must he have felt, coming home and finding her here, installed in his home, enjoying the life that he had given up because of her?

And poor Mamma Cristina was carrying the weight of all that guilt—which was only partially hers!

"It's not your fault that Davide went to sea," Eleonora croaked.

"Of course it is."

"No, it's not. It's the fault of the girl Davide gave up the trattoria for. After what he had sacrificed, he should still be with her. Instead, she broke his heart and left him."

"How do you know?" Mamma Cristina asked.

As they locked gazes, Eleonora saw the moment Mamma Cristina understood.

"That girl is you?"

Eleonora nodded.

"I married Davide then divorced him."

Mamma Cristina blanched.

Oh no, she shouldn't have dropped such an emotional bombshell on Mamma Cristina when she was convalescent from heart problems!

"What's going on?" Davide's voice came from the swing doors.

Chapter 17

Davide

Davide marched into the kitchen.

Even if he hadn't known Eleonora and Mamma as well as he did, he could tell that something was wrong. The cutlets were abandoned half-breaded on the counter, Eleonora and Mamma were staring at each other and Mamma was as white as flour. Wasn't it enough for Eleonora to be stealing from his mother without trying to kill her too?

"What's my mum doing here when she's supposed to rest?" he challenged Eleonora.

"Are you okay?" he asked his mother, taking her wrist and checking for her pulse as she sat on a chair, in the middle of the room.

"Yes," his mother said so quietly it was a whisper.

"Why did you bring her down to work? She needs rest," Davide reproached Eleonora.

"I'm fine. She didn't do anything. I came down

of my own accord, and certainly not to work," Mamma said.

Her tone was strange. Something had happened. Had Mamma come down to check on Eleonora and caught her up to mischief? Eleonora was pale too.

"I came to persuade Eleonora to marry you," Mamma said candidly. "But I discovered that she already had."

Now it was Davide's turn to feel the blood draining from his face.

Eleonora had told her. He turned to her but she had the decency to avoid his gaze. She knew that she was guilty. She should have consulted him before revealing a secret that belonged to them both. But as he was discovering what kind of person she was, he shouldn't be surprised that she hadn't shown him that courtesy.

"I'm sorry, sweetheart. I was blinded by fear of losing you, but my fear made me lose you all the more! I can't blame you for getting married in secret. If only I'd had a chance to know Eleonora back then, I would have completely understood why you wanted to marry her and I would have given you my heartfelt blessing! Can you forgive me?"

Davide had fully forgiven his mother the moment he had received the call from the hospital. Faced with the prospect of losing her forever, all their arguments and resentments had paled into oblivion.

It was a pity that she had now fallen in love

with such a deceitful woman. But this was a conversation he'd need to have with her in private, away from Eleonora.

He squeezed Mamma Cristina's shoulder.

"I've already forgiven you."

"Thank you."

She had regained colour and looked better now, but she was clearly still troubled. She looked from one to the other.

"But why did you divorce?"

Davide nodded at Eleonora to go ahead with the explanations. She had started the revelations and she could continue. In fact, he was quite curious to hear her version of the events.

"It's complicated," she said.

That was a cowardly way to get out of the question, and he wanted to challenge her, but then he thought about his mother. She wasn't supposed to be put through all these emotions in her condition.

So he bit his tongue and said, "Let's talk about it another time. You've had enough emotions for one day. Let's take you back upstairs to rest, Mamma."

She looked sadly at him, which made his heart ache.

"I wish someone had invented a machine to turn back time," she said.

"You're not the first person to wish for that," he said, and realised that he had wished for it too.

Eleonora returned to her work on the cutlets with eagerness and he accompanied his mother up the stairs.

She looked weary and he felt sorry for her. Her dream of seeing him with Eleonora couldn't have been shattered more successfully.

He accompanied her to her chair. The twins were glued to the TV in the same way he had been as a child, on that same sofa.

"You can leave me now, sweetheart," Mamma Cristina said to him, then lowered her voice, "Go back downstairs and have a good talk with Eleonora. Maybe things can be patched up between you…"

She looked up hopefully at him. He had been wrong: his mother had not lost her hopes after all.

"Yes, I'm going downstairs to talk to her," he said.

But he was not intending to patch anything up at all.

Chapter 18

Eleonora

Eleonora kept wiping the worktop over and over. Really, she needed a brisk walk to use up all the adrenaline from that conversation, but it was still raining and she'd have to open the trattoria to the lunch customers soon.

When they were still together, Davide had loved her more than she had realised, to the point of giving up his family, his trattoria and his town. But now he seemed to hate her more than he had any reason for, even accusing her of wanting to kill his mother.

She pushed the thought away and tried to concentrate on the bread she was cutting and putting into baskets. She would soon have to smile for customers.

"What game are you playing?" Davide's voice came from behind her.

She turned around slowly. He looked very upset.

"What do you mean?"

"What could have possibly made you decide that this was a good time to tell Mamma? You've been here for two years. Why didn't you make your big revelation before?"

He was right.

"I'm sorry. I should have discussed this with you before breaking the news to Mamma Cristina. But I had to tell her because she was blaming herself for things that are not her fault. It was the right moment."

"The right moment for what—to kill her?"

There was that accusation again. It really hurt her because, after her daughters, Eleonora loved Mamma Cristina more than anyone else on earth.

"I really didn't mean to hurt her—"

"Isn't stealing from her enough? Why do you hate us so much?" Davide interrupted, a runaway emotional bulldozer.

"Stealing?"

"Did you think I would never notice the money that's missing from the trattoria's account?"

"I don't know what you're talking about."

"I already knew you were unreliable but I always thought you were sincere. When you changed your mind about having kids—then, clearly, changed your mind again—I thought you had done it in good faith, not to trick me. But I was wrong about you all along. Now I can finally see that you are a deceitful witch."

Even in their worst arguments near the end of

their marriage, he had never called her a "deceitful witch".

"What's happening to you? Where is all this poison coming from?" she asked.

"All I want is one piece of truth from you—just one. Why are you bent on destroying my family?"

"I can't recognise this monster in front of me!"

Their voices must have grown loud enough to be heard upstairs because the girls appeared at the bottom of the stairs.

"Where is the monster?" Violetta asked.

"There's no monster, sweethearts. Go back upstairs," Eleonora said, trying to make her voice sound like usual.

"I'm sorry, I tried to keep them upstairs," Mamma Cristina said, peeking out too.

Oh no, she was tiring herself going up and down those stairs, and her eyes were shiny as if she had been crying. Eleonora knew she had only herself to blame for this. She should have kept her mouth shut!

Just then, Davide's phone rang. He pulled it out of his pocket impatiently, as if intending to stop it ringing and drop it back into his pocket. But when he saw the display, he took the call.

"Hello Attilio, you've been quick," he said aloud, putting the phone on speaker.

Why did he want her to listen to this conversation? Who was Attilio?

"The fraud department works fast. Every second's delay could cost the bank thousands of euros," Attilio said.

Ah yes, Attilio was the bank manager. Was this something to do with Davide's accusations that she had stolen something?

"Good to know. What news have you got for me? Good ones?"

"Whether they're good or bad, that's for you to decide. But I know who's made all those cash withdrawals. Every one of them."

Chapter 19

Davide

"Who?" Davide asked expectantly.

He wasn't sure what he was hoping for. He didn't want it to be Eleonora. A part of him still wanted to believe that she was honest and good, and that she had always told him the truth. Because if that wasn't the case, she could have lied to him even when she told him that she loved him.

All these years, he had put the failure of their marriage down to the children issue. He and Eleonora had loved each other but they had discovered that their life plans were incompatible and had had to part. But if Eleonora was a thief and a liar, maybe even those early times in their relationship had been an illusion. She had never loved him.

But another part of him wanted to discover who had stolen the money so that he could protect Mamma from more harm. And if that person wasn't Eleonora, who could it be?

On the other side of the phone, Attilio cleared his voice.

"It was your mum."

Davide felt as if the ground was rocking under his feet. His gaze flew to his mother, who looked down at her feet, her guilty demeanour confirming Attilio's words.

"Thank you, Attilio," Davide said, recovering his voice.

"It's okay. If you need anything more, let me know."

His friend sounded sympathetic. In his job, he must have seen lots of troubles within families due to money.

"Girls, go back upstairs and play on your own," Eleonora told the twins, then turned to Mamma. "It's time to open the restaurant. Shall I?"

"Yes, please," Mamma croaked, then looked up at Davide like a child waiting for punishment.

But it wasn't punishment that Davide wanted. It was explanations.

"Why did you take so much cash out of the bank that we're in overdraft? What did you use it for?" he asked her.

"Let's go to the office," she said with a sigh.

Davide's hopes that there would be a simple, understandable answer, vanished.

He closed the door of the tiny room and Mamma slumped into her chair. He remained standing, too tense to sit down.

"Now, there's nothing to worry about," she started—which worried him.

"I'm not in any trouble and I can look after myself very well," she continued, which worried him even more.

"It's not as bad as it looks—"

"Mamma, please, come to the point."

"A new customer started coming to the trattoria. He told me he enjoyed my food very much and he wanted to protect my trattoria from all the criminals around. He said that businesses without protection can encounter many problems, and he offered to protect the trattoria in exchange for a small monthly payment and free meals. I agreed and he's been coming once a month to collect the money and eat. Nothing bad," she explained with a tentative smile.

Did she really believe that the man's offer was an innocent and legitimate security contract? Was she trying to convince him of that, or perhaps herself?

"Mamma, this man is not protecting you from criminals. He and his clan are the criminals. The way he's 'protecting' you is that his clan won't burn the trattoria down so long as you pay him. This is racketeering and extortion."

She looked at her clasped hands.

"Well, I did wonder about that. But there was no point in digging into it too much. The result was the same. If I didn't pay him, I would have continued having problems."

"What problems?"

"There have been some acts of vandalism, that's why we've had to refurbish."

Now it all made sense. He had unjustly accused Eleonora of masterminding the trattoria's refurbishment to bankrupt it, but he had been completely wrong. As he had been about the mysterious cash withdrawals.

Mamma and Eleonora had had to deal with all this on their own, while he was blissfully sailing the oceans.

"Why didn't you tell me?" he asked.

"You were far away and I didn't want to trouble you. There was nothing you could do."

"I could have given you advice."

Now it was too late to recover all the money that was lost.

"So you've been withdrawing all that cash to pay him, is that correct?"

"Yes. It started with small sums but recently his fees have gone up."

"Enough to send a healthy business into overdraft," Davide said wryly.

"It's been so gradual that I didn't notice it becoming too much."

"One cent would have been too much. This man has no right to take your money or demand free meals. You should have gone to the police as soon as he asked."

"I thought about it but I decided that it was too stressful—filling in forms, giving statements…

And would the police manage to keep us safe? We were two women with children, all on our own."

Davide felt a pang of guilt. If he hadn't gone to sea, he would have been there to protect them and to fill in the forms at the police station. He would have been there to send the man away and call in the support of the anti-extortion associations.

"You think I've been weak and cowardly—" Mamma said.

"I don't."

"—but I was busy and I wanted to get on with my job. Paying the thug to go away and leave me in peace was easier and quicker than dealing with the problem through the police. I now realise that I was only putting off the problem and making it bigger. Paying the money certainly didn't give me the peace of heart I thought it would."

Davide thought about her heart attack. The stress of the extortion must have contributed to it. Anger against the racketeers mixed with his guilt for leaving mamma alone.

"We're going to the police now, then we'll pay a visit to Alice's mother, Renata. She stood up against the 'protection money' racket and founded an association to help other local businesses do the same."

Mamma's eyes lit up.

"I never knew that! Aren't you a wonderful son? I'm so lucky to have you."

Davide sighed. This was the most undeserved praise he had ever received.

Chapter 20

Eleonora

Eleonora locked up the trattoria and padded upstairs.

Thankfully, the trattoria had been quiet tonight—it must have been the rain—so she had easily been able to manage on her own and even put the girls to bed when the last customers were eating.

She dropped onto the armchair by the balcony. She felt shattered.

From the moment she had found the paparazzo waiting for her in Mamma's car, it had been an emotional screw press of a day, with Davide's accusations being the last, horrible, squeeze.

Even if the bank manager's phone call had cleared her from Davide's suspicions of theft, she was still shaken by the fact that Davide had so easily believed her to be the culprit. He had believed that she could steal from the woman she loved most, or that she would want to kill her with her emotional revelations.

Clearly Davide was convinced that she had sought a job at Mamma Cristina's because of some sinister plan.

To be fair, it must be difficult for anyone to believe that she had wanted to give her daughters a surrogate grandma, if they didn't know that Mamma Cristina was the girls' real grandma.

She must tell Mamma Cristina the truth as soon as possible, and certainly before the paparazzo did it for her.

Mamma Cristina was sure to be delighted to be the twin's grandma, and Eleonora would have told her in a heartbeat. But that meant telling Davide too. It was too big a secret to ask a mother to keep from her son. Anyway, Mamma Cristina was unable to keep secrets.

So Eleonora had to tell Davide too.

This was the part she dreaded. It would have been a lot easier if she had told him as soon as she found out she was pregnant. Unfortunately, she was stopped by her own pride and the fear that he would insist on remaining married—after today's exchanges, she was sure she shouldn't have worried about that.

She looked out the window into the darkness. The lighthouse's rotating beam of light struggled to push through the night and the wind rattled the windows, bringing the smell of the sea into the flat.

Davide and Mamma Cristina were still out.

What were they up to? Eleonora hoped that Mamma wasn't in trouble with the bank. Or with Davide. Eleonora didn't know which would be worse.

She could see how he might have checked the trattoria's account books, recognised Eleonora's handwriting and come to the wrong conclusions about her. But it still hurt her that he could have thought her a thief.

A car's headlights flickered through the trees at the bottom of the hill. It must be Davide and Mamma coming back.

Eleonora retreated to her room. Once Mamma Cristina had gone to bed, Eleonora would try and catch Davide on his own to tell him the truth about the twins. Then there would be no more secrets between then, and they could discuss how to tell Mamma Cristina.

Eleonora lay on her bed and closed her eyes, focusing on her hearing.

She heard the key turning slowly into the front door's lock, the ginger steps of Davide and Mamma Cristina, whispering to each other so as not to wake her and the girls. Eleonora was a little surprised by such consideration on Davide's part after the way he had attacked her earlier.

Eleonora waited until she heard Mamma Cristina's door click shut, then she padded out of her room and into the corridor.

Davide was nowhere to be seen. No light came from under his bedroom door, nor from under the bathroom door. He had vanished.

Eleonora heard noises downstairs. He must be in the office. She pulled a cardigan over her pyjamas and headed downstairs.

The office was dark but the kitchen light was on. Davide must be there, struck by late-night hunger. Eleonora pushed through the swing doors.

Davide wasn't eating. He was taking some dough out of a cupboard where it must have been proving.

Eleonora hadn't used that cupboard recently and she had no idea that he was using it. When had he put that dough there? She hadn't seen him. He must have deliberately avoided her. Maybe he always worked in the kitchen at night as a way to avoid her. This was how much he hated and mistrusted her, she thought sadly.

Her resolve faltered. Maybe she should try to regain his trust before breaking the news of the girls' paternity. She should turn around and go back to her room before he saw her. But she couldn't. She was transfixed.

All those years ago, she had fallen in love with him when she had seen him cook. Now she couldn't help but watch him. His movements were so gentle. He treated the food with respect. To her surprise, she still enjoyed watching him at work.

He lay the dough gently on the worktop, separated it into portions and weighed them carefully, then put each into a mould. Eleonora recognised the shape of pandoro moulds.

The traditional northern-Italian Christmas cake was notoriously laborious to prepare, involving several rounds of proving. If he was putting the doughs into the mould tonight, he must have already done all the other proving cycles during previous nights—all these times making sure she wouldn't see him. Knowing that he had gone to such lengths to avoid her made her heart ache. She was about to turn away and pad back upstairs, when he turned and saw her.

"Oh. Hello."

He didn't sound angry or gruff. Just surprised.

"Hello. I didn't mean to disturb you. Sorry."

"It's okay. Were you looking for something?"

"No... Just checking for burglars. I'm going back up. Goodnight," she said.

"I'm sorry for accusing you earlier."

"I can see how you could have jumped to conclusions, knowing that I've been doing the trattoria's accounts. But I must confess that this level of mistrust was still hurtful," she said honestly.

"You haven't given me any reason to trust you, Eleonora. In fact, the contrary."

"Why?"

He put the dough back down on the worktop.

"I saw you this morning in the car with the paparazzo," he said icily.

"Then why didn't you come and help me?"

"Help you give him information?"

It took Eleonora a few seconds to understand.

"You thought that I was giving him information?"

"You shook hands."

Sadness and disappointment swept over her. How could he think that she would be in cahoots with that man?

"And you didn't give me the benefit of the doubt," she said sadly.

"He was in Mamma's car with you."

"Couldn't you imagine that he might not have been invited?"

Eleonora saw understanding dawn on Davide's face, then the same expression he had when he had chased the paparazzo the first time the man had troubled her.

"I'm sorry. I should have got out of the car and helped you," he said, looking genuinely sorry.

"I can see how it looked. I told him I'd give him information and confirmed that the wedding was still planned for the 14th of April. This way, I can feed him false information and keep him off our backs."

"I'm sorry if I've doubted you."

"You haven't doubted me once. You've doubted me many times," she said.

She wanted to say "accused" instead of "doubted", but she didn't want to be too confrontational.

"Each time new suspicions arose, they seemed to confirm the old ones."

"I understand. You came back and found me here without a convincing reason for my strange choice. You discovered that I was doing the trattoria's accounts and then that money was missing. You knew I had been approached by a paparazzo and next thing we were shaking hands. A string of unfortunate coincidences."

"I was wrong about the missing money, and I appreciate your honesty about the paparazzo. But I still haven't understood why you've decided that the mother of your ex-husband is the best person to be a grandmotherly figure for your daughters."

This was the time to tell him that the girls were his daughters. Eleonora swallowed, preparing herself for the revelation and Davide's reaction.

But Davide continued.

"The more I go around the village, the more I find that everyone thinks the world of you. I shouldn't have doubted you. You've been honest with me all along, and you know that I value honesty above all."

Eleonora's resolve drained. How could she tell him that she had lied to him about the girls' paternity —or not told him the truth—when he'd just praised her honesty? She had only just regained his trust.

"You look tired," he said kindly. "You've done a great job holding the fort since Mamma got ill. Whatever your reasons for coming here, I can see that you love her very much."

"Yes, I do."

"At least, that's one thing we can agree on."
"That's right. Goodnight, Davide."
"Goodnight, Eleonora."

Chapter 21

Davide

Thankfully yesterday's storm had let up and Davide could work on the restaurant's terrace.

The wedding was approaching fast and the terrace needed some repairs before it could host Paolo and Alice's guests—weather permitting. Also, Davide needed some time on his own, and outside was the only place he could be away from his mum and Eleonora.

He found some cement and sand in the garage and mixed them with water in a bucket to make mortar. He carried bucket and trowel outside to the stairs with the wobbly step. He lifted the stone that had come loose, cleaned it of moss and debris, scraped off the old mortar and replaced the stone over a new bed of mortar.

Next job was to ensure all the outdoor tables and chairs were in working order. He looked up and discovered he had company. Violetta and Veronica were sitting on the top step, watching him.

"Hello," he greeted them with a smile.

He enjoyed their company, even when he felt like being on his own. For some reason, the girls had quickly grown on him. Maybe it was because he had always liked children—which was one of the reasons he had wanted them so much.

Or maybe it was the girls' candour and honesty. Mamma Cristina had kept secrets from him. He had kept secrets from her. And Eleonora...Heaven only knew how many secrets she was keeping from him!

But these girls were refreshing. With them, what he saw was what he got.

"Hello. What are you doing?" they asked him.

"I'm fixing things. Like this wobbly step."

"Why didn't Mummy fix it?"

"I don't think she noticed. She's very busy in the kitchen."

"Is it because boys mix cement and girls mix flour?"

"No. Boys can mix flour and girls can mix cement. Everyone can mix what they like. I love mixing flour," he said.

He had done it every night since he had arrived —mixing the dough for the pandoro which would be his surprise present for Paolo and Alice.

He'd had to feed the starter dough four times before even starting the pandoro dough. Then he mixed flour, eggs, starter dough and butter in stages. He let it leaven and repeated the whole process twice more, adding icing sugar and more eggs and butter laced with rum, vanilla seeds and cocoa butter. He had done all this in the middle of the night so that he didn't get in anyone else's way. Also, so that nobody else would know about his pandoro.

There was no good reason he should be secretive about it, but since Eleonora had wedged herself into his home and his town, he had felt the need to keep something to himself—some privacy and space of his own.

"Mummy says you are a cook too."

Davide wished he could know what else their mummy said about him, but he didn't want to ask. He was not going to take advantage of the girls to find out information about their mum.

"Yes, I am."

"Why don't we ever see you in the kitchen?"

Davide guessed that this one was Veronica. He was starting to be able to tell them apart from their behaviours.

"Because Mummy is bossy: she never lets us play in the kitchen," Violetta answered her sister.

Davide smiled at the way Violetta assumed that, if they weren't allowed, obviously why should he? It was sweet the way children kept adults humble. He was going to miss them when Eleonora left.

A thought came to him. Did Eleonora have to leave? Why couldn't she stay, now that she had been cleared of all the crimes he had suspected her of?

Now that Mamma knew about their past and would stop matchmaking, living under the same roof might be okay. Surely they could be grown up enough to share the trattoria and Mamma without letting the past get in their way and cause trouble.

He was still baffled by Eleonora's decision to take up work at his Mamma's trattoria, but he was now reasonably confident that she didn't have sinister intentions.

"Can we help you?" Violetta asked him.

"Why not? If I put out the chairs and the tables, you could wipe them."

"Yes!" the girls chorused as if they had just won the lottery.

He gave them buckets, sponges and his gloves. But as soon as the girls put on his gloves —one hand each—it was clear that they were way too big for them.

"Wait here and I'll go and get some smaller ones," he said.

Hoping he hadn't underestimated the mischief two children could make with a bucket and some sponges, he left the girls and jogged to the kitchen.

"Have you seen the girls?" Eleonora asked him as soon as he entered, looking up at him without stopping her fast chopping.

She was still as talented as he remembered.

"Yes. They're with me."

Her expression changed for a moment, and he couldn't tell if it was a good or a bad change.

"They want to help me so I've asked them to

wipe the tables and chairs, if that's okay with you?"

"Of course. You don't have to ask me," she said as if, for some reason, he could have taken that permission for granted.

"Thanks. I'm looking for some small gloves for them. Mine are too big for —"

He was about to say the girls' ages but realised he didn't know. He could end the sentence with the words "children" or "little girls", but Davide realised that this was his chance to ask Eleonora their age.

He hadn't asked the girls or Mamma because that had felt underhanded. But it would be perfectly fair to find out from Eleonora.

"—three-year-olds?"

The girls looked older than three, but he purposefully said a number that was far off so that Eleonora would correct him.

"Of course. I'll find something smaller," she said, heading for the cleaning cupboard.

His plan hadn't worked. She hadn't corrected him even if the girls were clearly older. On one occasion, Elenora had mentioned Christmas holiday homework so the girls must be old enough to attend some form of schooling. Was Eleonora deliberately avoiding the subject?

That thought made him want to know the answer even more. The one way to find out was to swallow his pride and ask.

Eleonora returned with some small rubber gloves.

"How old are the girls?"

He tried to sound casual.

Panic flitted across Eleonora's face and she hesitated for a moment, but then quickly recovered her guard.

"Four," she answered without meeting his gaze, and handed him the gloves.

"Thanks."

As he walked back towards the girls, Davide did some mental maths. Eleonora must have got together with the girls' father very quickly after their divorce.

Chapter 22

Eleonora

Eleonora weighed the "00" flour to make the fileja pasta. A type of maccheroni made with a metal rod, this typical Calabrian pasta, dressed with a wild boar ragù sauce, was going to be the first course of Paolo and Alice's wedding, like a traditional Christmas lunch.

Making enough for the wedding party was going to require a lot of work, and Eleonora wasn't going to leave it to the last minute. But thankfully, the pasta kept well in the fridge, so she had already started making it.

She mixed the flour with water until she got the right texture, then rolled the dough into a long fat worm, cut it into sections and rolled those again into strings.

She pressed a metal rod into the middle of the string, rolling it a little to create a cavity, then rested the finished pasta on a floured tray, and repeated it all over again.

Mamma Cristina was much faster. She could make the pasta at the rate of one string per verse of the song "Volare".

Eleonora started singing the song. She couldn't quite produce the pasta at the same rate as Mamma, but she still enjoyed the song's open vowels, the happy tune, the cheerful words.

"I thought so," Mamma Cristina's voice came from the stairs. She emerged with a smile. "I thought that, if you were singing 'Volare', you must be making fileja," she said.

Eleonora smiled. It was nice to feel that, even if she was upstairs, Mamma Cristina watched over everyone.

Mamma came up to the worktop and rolled up her sleeves.

"No, Mamma. You need to rest."

"Nonsense. I've rested enough. Any more rest and I will end up resting forever, six feet under."

She floured her hands and rolled some dough.

"Davide will be cross with me," Eleonora protested weakly.

As well as speeding up production, Mamma's help meant she would keep Eleonora company, which Eleonora enjoyed a lot.

"Let him complain as much as he wants. We don't want patriarchy anymore, do we?"

Eleonora smiled.

"Indeed not."

They worked in companionable silence— rolling, pressing, lifting the dough—in the way people who are really close to each other can do without feeling any awkwardness.

"Have I been the only stumbling block between you two?" Mamma asked, suddenly.

Eleonora stopped rolling and turned to look at her.

"You are not a stumbling block between us."

Mamma kept rolling.

"Maybe not now but certainly I have been," she said quietly. "I was the one who didn't want him to marry a non-Altavician girl. He had to hide you away and marry you in secret. I can't begin to imagine how upsetting that must have been for you, to feel so rejected by your mother-in-law before you'd even met her. I was so stupid, so narrow-minded!"

Mamma's shoulders folded inwards, curling her like a withering leaf.

Eleonora hugged her.

"We all make mistakes. Heaven knows I've made mine too."

Mamma looked up at her with sad, watery eyes.

"If you're talking about divorcing Davide, I'm sure I contributed to that too," Mamma said, her voice quivering.

It was sweet that Mamma Cristina thought that Eleonora considered divorcing Davide one of her mistakes. In truth, maybe it was.

"You can't blame yourself for everything, Mamma. And no, Davide and I didn't fall out because of you. Yes, I was sad that he was keeping me a secret from his family and his village. I was sad that we couldn't have a proper wedding and celebrate with all our friends and family. But this wasn't the reason why we divorced."

"What was it, then?" Mamma asked with big puppy eyes, still holding onto Eleonora's hug.

If anyone could ask Eleonora such a personal question, it had to the woman she loved like a mother. She let go of Mamma, leaving floury handprints on her arms and back.

"We disagreed over having children."

Mamma's eyes widened with surprise.

"But Davide has always liked children."

"I was the one who didn't want them."

Eleonora looked away and resumed rolling the dough.

"But you've had the girls. Did you change your mind?"

"The girls were a surprise. But I've loved them from the moment I knew about them."

Mamma sighed.

"What a pity that it happened too late for Davide...or maybe it's not too late," Mamma said, her eyes brightening. "You could still get back together and be a family. I'm sure Davide won't mind that the girls aren't his. I've seen how he talks to them, plays with them, looks at them. I can tell that he loves them."

Eleonora avoided her gaze. She must not tell Mamma Cristina that the girls were Davide's before she told him. Anyway, this was not what was keeping them apart.

"Too much has happened between us. We could never start again. We can be friends," Eleonora conceded, even though she wasn't sure about that.

He still didn't fully trust her, and she still found him attractive, both of which weren't good grounds for a friendship.

Mamma Cristina looked at her hopefully.

"You could have a proper wedding this time. I would make mountains of fileja, cook a feast for you with all my heart."

"I know you would," Eleonora said, hugging her again.

The two women held tight onto each other for a little longer, until Violetta and Veronica returned with their buckets and sponges.

"Look, Mummy and Mamma Cristina have been playing with flour!"

Chapter 23

Davide

Davide had fixed the awning and the umbrellas, the girls had wiped the tables and the chairs, and together they had strung more fairy lights around the garden than there were in the whole of Altavicia's town centre.

Violetta and Veronica had turned out to be more helpful than he had imagined. They were very mature for their age.

Davide had thought of buying them dolls for Christmas but now, having seen them at work, he thought that a craft kit might be more appropriate. They had their nimble fingers and an eagerness to learn that reminded him of their mother.

Maybe he could teach them some of the sailors' knots he had learnt on the yacht. He could even show them how to make a rope ladder.

But maybe he was dreaming to have that time to spend with them. Christmas was going to be very busy with the wedding and any drama that might come with it if the paparazzi got wind of it. Or if Eleonora had told them, he thought, then immediately chased that thought away. He wanted to trust Eleonora again.

He went to the office to check the trattoria's emails.

There was one from Renata asking how they were. Last night, she had given them lots of good advice on how to deal with the "protection" racket. The man who had been extorting money from Mamma Cristina hadn't turned up for this month's "fees" yet, but there were good chances he would before Christmas.

Davide fired back a quick email to reassure her that their morale was still high and their resolution to resist the criminal hadn't wavered.

Then there was an email from Paolo, checking on the wedding preparations. Davide confirmed that the wine had been delivered, the dry food supplies were all in, and the terrace was ready and would be available to guests if the weather was good.

Paolo had ended his email with the P.S, "Do you remember when we used to swim on Christmas Day?"

Davide remembered. From the age of fourteen, when their parents felt they couldn't stop them any longer, he and Paolo used to meet at the beach on Christmas morning after church but before filling their stomachs with their families' Christmas lunch feasts. And they would swim.

Some years, the weather had been warm, sunny and very inviting. Other years, the wind had lashed them and the rain had stung them but, by then, their Christmas swim had become a tradition so they had gone ahead anyway.

Was Paolo suggesting they did it again? Surely not this Christmas—the day of his wedding!

"Yes, I remember. Those were good times," Davide typed back.

There were no more jobs for him to do in the office. All the remaining wedding preparations were to be done in the kitchen.

Until now, Davide had avoided the kitchen and Eleonora and had found plenty of other jobs to do outside it, but now he had run out. Instead, there were large quantities of food to prepare for the wedding feast.

He couldn't avoid Eleonora forever.

He powered off the computer, pushed the chair under the desk and headed for the kitchen.

Chapter 24

Eleonora

Eleonora and Mamma had finished preparing the pasta and had put it away in the fridge. They had refreshed the starter dough which they would need for the nacatole doughnuts, and had started cutting some soft dried figs in half to make little crosses covered in sugar and baked, the crucitti, another local Christmas sweet.

A grunt came from the walk-in fridge. A little later, Davide emerged, carrying a skinned boar on his shoulders.

He looked strong, rough and handsome, and Eleonora's heart skipped a beat. It had taken two men to carry it from the butcher's van to the trattoria's fridge. Davide was handling it all on his own, and very successfully.

He put it down on the worktop to prepare it. They were going to roast it slowly on a spit, but first it needed to be marinated.

Davide stretched and twisted his back.

"Are you okay?" Eleonora asked, trying to keep the worry out of her voice.

"Just a little shorter," he joked.

"That's okay, then. You're tall enough," his mother said. "And I'm glad you put a kitchen towel on your shoulders."

Then she turned to Eleonora.

"I'll finish the figs. You help him."

Eleonora wondered if this was another matchmaking attempt. Mamma Cristina wasn't a woman who gave up easily.

"I don't need help," Davide said.

"You do," Mamma insisted. "Someone needs to turn the boar while the other person bastes it."

Mamma was right, and it was a no-brainer who should be turning the boar and who should be basting it.

Eleonora took a wide brush and the bowl of marinade and started spreading the thick glossy liquid onto the skin while Davide made access easy for her.

They hadn't cooked together for years and she was surprised at how well they worked as a team. They didn't need words. Each could tell what the other was about to do from the smallest movement of a wrist, or the position of the body.

Davide glanced at Eleonora's flour-dusted clothes.

"Did you and my mother fight over a bag of flour?" he asked with a deadpan expression but

Eleonora could see a smile playing at the corner of his lips.

"We had a flour-fight," she joked, winking at Mamma Cristina only to discover that the cheeky woman had abandoned her workstation and left them alone.

"What's that?"

"The kitchen equivalent of a pillow-fight."

Davide smiled and Eleonora's heart flipped. She hadn't seen him smile at her in years. Since he'd come back to Altavicia, she had seen him smile at his mum, at Paolo, even at the girls. But not once had he smiled at her. She had forgotten the warm glow in her chest his smile used to give her—and, surprisingly, still did.

"Yes, you've always liked a hearty pillow-fight," he said, avoiding her gaze.

Memories flooded back to Eleonora. At the beginning of their marriage, they used to play a lot. Small competitions, gentle teasing, little pranks that always ended with a kiss. They enjoyed saying sorry and granting forgiveness to each other.

"Yes, I did," she said, her voice coming out more nostalgic than she had intended.

An awkward silence fell between them. Davide broke it, changing the topic.

"I'm not sure I enjoy roasting animals anymore."

"Same here. As I'm getting older, I'm feeling sorrier for the animals."

"You're not old, Eleonora. You're only thirty."

He had remembered her age and had calculated how old she was now.

Eleonora glanced up and met his gaze. It was only one moment of distraction, but enough to send her basting brush up his hand.

"I'm sorry!"

She dropped the brush and tried to wipe the oil off the top of his hand with hers. As soon as she felt his skin—so familiar, never forgotten—she couldn't let go.

They remained like this—hand on top of hand, eyes locked together. His intense blue eyes were scrambling her thoughts, sending her reason away. All she could feel was the connection between them. It had never gone away. Could he feel it too?

After what felt like an age, the noise of the girls running back in snapped her out of it and she retracted her hand as if she had been burnt.

"I think this boar has been basted enough," she croaked, wiped her hands on her apron and returned to her workstation.

Chapter 25

Davide

Davide hastily put the boar away to marinate and retreated back to the office.

Stepping into the kitchen had been mistake. Just half an hour in there with Eleonora had catapulted him back years. That feeling of closeness and connection while they cooked together... he had forgotten how nice it could feel.

And he still found Eleonora attractive. This was dangerous. Nothing good could come out of it, only more suffering.

No matter how much his mother wished they got back together, there was no future for them. He and Eleonora had hurt each other too much. Mistakes had been made that couldn't be undone, words had been said that could not be unsaid, and trust had been shattered in a way that it couldn't be pieced back together.

The damage caused by their short relationship had been so deep that not only could he not love

Eleonora again as a wife, but he would never love anyone else either.

He sat at the desk and turned on the laptop.

Paolo had replied. He was pleased with the progress of the wedding preparations and suggested a Boxing Day swim to celebrate surviving the wedding day and to carry on their Christmas tradition, even if one day later.

Paolo continued saying that he hoped Davide didn't mind Alice joining them too. He also suggested—and here Davide had to read the sentence again—that Eleonora joined them as well.

Was Paolo suggesting this so that Davide didn't feel like the gooseberry? Or was Paolo, too, trying to set them up?

Now that Mamma Cristina knew about his past with Eleonora, he should tell his friend too. Paolo was going to be upset with him for keeping this secret, but he would be even more upset if he found out from Eleonora rather than from him.

At least, Paolo already knew that he had got married in secret. All that was left for him to know was that Eleonora was the woman.

Davide got up and searched for his woolly hat. Since he had shaved his head, hats had become a necessity. He checked the shelves and the drawers. He finally found it under a pile of papers.

His gaze fell on a document. It was a school enrolment form for the twins. It might contain the name of the girls' father. Davide knew he should not read it, but Eleonora had left it in his office in plain view. He couldn't resist.

He scanned the top page, flicked to the second page and read to the end.

There was no name of father, but there was the girls' date of birth. And it didn't match what Eleonora had told him.

She had lied to him. The girls were older than four. Davide mentally calculated the years and months of their estrangement and divorce, pregnancy times and birth dates. There was only one conclusion he could draw. It was staring at him painfully. Eleonora must have cheated on him.

He slumped on the chair, hurt filling his chest.

Why would she do that to him? He had wanted children and she had denied them to him. Instead, while they were still together, she had gone and had children with someone else. Why would she have hated him so much?

He had to talk to someone or he'd lose his sanity thinking about it. One more reason to pay Paolo a visit and fill him in on everything.

Davide found Paolo at home alone.

"Is everything alright?" Paolo asked as soon as he saw Davide's face.

"Not really, but don't worry: it's nothing to do with your wedding."

Paolo offered him a seat and a coffee, but Davide could only stomach a glass of water.

They sat in front of the patio doors, with a view to the pretty little garden, and a plate of Paolo's mum's homemade *mostaccioli* biscuits.

"You know that I secretly got married and then divorced," Davide started.

"Yes. A few years ago, right?"

"Yes. Well, what I didn't tell you is that my ex-wife is Eleonora."

Paolo froze, one hand holding a *mostacciolo* midair.

"No way! Is this why she's working at your mum's trattoria?"

"I have no idea why she's working at my mum's trattoria. I didn't know she had applied for a job there and my mum didn't know who she was when she hired her. As far as Mamma was concerned, she had employed a complete stranger. Eleonora didn't tell her until yesterday."

The mostacciolo finally got into Paolo's mouth.

"So you got the shock of your life when you came home and found her there."

"Precisely. That was a few minutes before you and Alice walked in."

"That explains why you looked bewildered. I thought it was because of the stress of your mother's illness. But why did you divorce?"

"We disagreed about children."

"I thought you wanted them."

"She didn't."

"So the girls weren't planned?"

"I have no idea."

"Well, in any case, congratulations. You've got two lovely daughters!"

"Paolo, you don't understand. The girls aren't mine."

Paolo frowned in confusion.

"Quite right, I don't understand. Your ex-wife has come to work and live with your mum with her daughters who aren't yours. And she didn't want children but you did."

Davide nodded.

"Correct. We argued so much over having children that we divorced. It doesn't make sense, does it?"

"Do you have any idea how old the girls are?"

Davide wasn't going to admit to memorising their dates of birth.

"Too old to have been conceived after Eleonora and I separated," Davide grated out.

Saying the words out loud felt like spitting broken glass.

"Then they're undoubtedly yours," Paolo told him cheerfully, patting him on the back. "Congratulations!"

"Why would you think that?"

Davide had come to his friend to keep a grip on his own sanity but now it looked like his friend was losing his own.

"They look more like Eleonora, I'll grant you that. But they have a lot of you too. While I was having dinner in the trattoria with Alice, a few weeks ago, I watched them play. The way they stick out their tongue when they're concentrating, the way they hold their pencil, even the way they walk between the tables, trailing their hands over the legs of the tables—it all reminded me of you. I thought I was being nostalgic, seeing you in other children because I remembered us playing in the trattoria together. But now it all makes sense."

"No, it doesn't. If the girls were mine, why wouldn't Eleonora tell me?"

"That's for you to find out. It would certainly explain why Eleonora has come to live here with your mum. She's their grandma."

Davide's mind reeled. He hadn't seen himself in the girls, but that was because he hadn't looked. Had hadn't thought of that possibility for one moment. But if he was the girls' father and Mamma was their grandmother, Eleonora's strange explanations for coming to Altavicia made absolute sense.

Davide thanked his friend and said goodbye, despite Paolo's protests that he hadn't tasted even one mostacciolo.

Davide hurried back to the trattoria. He had left it to find peace and sanity but now he was coming back with more internal turmoil than before. And lots of new questions.

He must confront Eleonora, but not before

Paolo's wedding. Nothing must go wrong on his best friend's big day.

Chapter 26

Eleonora

Because of Paolo and Alice's wedding taking place on Christmas Day, Mamma Cristina suggested they celebrated Christmas on Christmas Eve.

She asked Eleonora and Davide to go along with her to Midnight Mass, and neither of them had the heart to disappoint her, even if Eleonora squirmed at the idea of what felt like a "family" trip.

Which was fully what Mamma Cristina had intended, as Eleonora could tell by watching her beam as she walked into the church with one girl at each hand and Eleonora and Davide following behind her, looking like a couple. Anyone who didn't know better would have easily assumed that they were.

The girls had loved the midnight outing and the ceremony with the incense, the organ and the crowd dressed up to the nines. After church, Eleonora and Mamma Cristina had given them their presents to make sure they wouldn't get up early the next day.

Now it was Christmas morning, the girls were fast asleep and the grownups were already hard at work on Paolo and Alice's wedding.

The doctor had finally given Mamma Cristina permission to return to the kitchen and she was busy with the final preparations.

To avoid alerting any paparazzi lurking around, all the deliveries had been put off to the last minute—today. Disgruntled delivery men in their vans had trundled up to the trattoria since early morning, impatient to return to their family on Christmas Day. Eleonora and Davide had got up after only a couple of hours' sleep and had been working flat out since.

But Eleonora was more than happy to do it. She loved Alice and Paolo and she was determined to give them the wedding she hadn't had.

She checked the last box of wedding favours which had just been delivered. Traditional sugar-coated almonds wrapped in tulle were tied to decorative ceramic pinecones believed to bring good luck and prosperity.

Eleonora checked that none of them was broken, then put them out on the table for the bride and the groom to distribute to their guests on arrival.

The ceramic pinecones looked great and appropriately Christmassy, but there weren't as many as she had expected and the table looked a little bare. It could do with some real pinecones from the garden and a few sprigs of pine with their lovely scent.

Eleonora headed out to the garden with some secateurs.

A delicate pink sun was just rising behind the purple sea, promising a mild sunny day. Then they would be able to make full use the terrace, she thought with a grin.

As she snipped a cone off a pine tree, she noticed something strange behind the drystone wall.

A thick black tube stuck out of a clump of diss grass. Eleonora tilted her head and the sun's light reflected off the end of the tube. It was a lens!

Paparazzi!

Her first instinct was to run up to the camera, confront whoever was hiding behind it, and tell them to go away.

But how long would it be before they came back? The land beyond the drystone wall was public land. Her reaction would only confirm that something worth capturing on camera was happening at the trattoria.

The best thing to do right now was to pretend she hadn't noticed, then tell Mamma Cristina and Davide in the hope that, between them, they could come up with a solution.

She took a steadying breath and walked back to the trattoria as if nothing had happened.

Davide was manning the spit.

"The hog roast is almost ready," he announced

with a grin.

Eleonora had noticed that, in the last few days, his mood changed. He seemed a lot more relaxed and, on occasions, he had even smiled at her.

The news of paparazzi on the other side of the wall was certainly going to dampen his mood. But she had to tell him.

"I think I've seen a camera's tele lens the other side of the wall," she said.

As she had expected, the smile drained from his face.

"How would they know?"

"I have no idea."

A glint of disbelief passed across his face and it sliced through Eleonora's heart. Was his trust in her so fragile that he could doubt her loyalty again?

"It wasn't me, Davide. I told you that I gave the man the wrong information," she said.

"You did, but you've also told too many lies. I don't know what to believe anymore."

He didn't sound angry, resentful or even disappointed. He just sounded weary, as if she had emotionally exhausted him.

He was right: she had lied to Mamma Cristina, to the entire town, and to him, even if he didn't know the extent of that yet. She had even lied to her own daughters, who called him "Mamma Cristina's boy" when they should call him "Daddy" instead.

But this wasn't about them. This was Paolo and Alice's wedding, and they had to pull together to protect it.

"It doesn't matter who told the paparazzi. If they're out here now, we need to do something about it," she said, her voice cracking a little.

"You're right." He thought for a moment. "I'll deal with it. You go out onto the terrace and pretend to prepare it for the wedding. Keep the paparazzi engaged."

"What are you planning to do?" she asked innocently.

He gave her a sharp look.

"That's all I want you to know."

He didn't trust her.

Chapter 27

Davide

D avide looked out the attic window. The same scooter that had hounded Eleonora up the hill days ago was parked further down the road, partially hidden behind a bush.

Pretending to fix some fairy lights, Davide paid a quick visit to the garden. The glass of a tele lens glinted in the diss grass, no doubt with a paparazzo behind it, just as Eleonora had told him.

Davide didn't know what to think of her. If she had grassed to the press, she wouldn't have come and told him about the tele lens. Unless, of course, he was being naïve and it was all part of a plan to divert the wedding somewhere else, where Paolo and Alice would be exposed to even more paparazzi.

In the uncertainty, keeping his new plan to himself had to be the wisest choice. But it didn't stop him feeling sad at the hurt look on her face when he refused to share the plan.

Paolo picked up at the first ring. He must have been just about to set off for the church—the little chapel outside town which wasn't used for regular services anymore.

"Everything alright?" Paolo asked.

"We've just spotted a paparazzo."

Paolo groaned.

"But I have plan," Davide reassured him.

"I'm all ears."

"The paparazzo doesn't know that we've seen him, so we're going to trick him."

"I like the sound of that. What do we do?"

"You wanted to have a festive swim, right?"

"What…?"

"Just listen. Mamma Cristina and I will take all the food and the entertainment down to the beach. All you have to do is tell your guests to go to the beach for the party instead of coming here."

"The mayor won't like that. I'm sure we need permission to put up an event on public land," Paolo objected.

"Nobody will make trouble for Luigi Felice's daughter on her wedding day. And, I dare say, the mayor will be delighted for you to bring publicity to our beautiful beach."

"The paparazzi will find out."

"Not if we keep them entertained at the trattoria."

"What do you mean?"

"We'll pretend that the wedding party is happening here. With respect, I doubt they'll be able to tell the difference between you and me through a tele lens."

Paolo chuckled.

"You are crazy, as always!"

That was a yes.

"By the way, as I'll be staying here with the paparazzi and I won't see you, I wish you a happy wedding and an even happier married life."

"Thank you."

Once that was sorted, Davide called the music band and instructed them to go to the beach instead of the trattoria. When they asked for the location's full address, Davide told them to look out for people and marquees.

Next, Davide counted the cars in the trattoria's car park. There were six, belonging to him, Mamma and the extra staff they had hired for the day. If these guys didn't mind, between them all they could transport all the food and drinks to the beach, as well as folding tables and chairs.

By now, the kitchen was buzzing with activity, with Mamma Cristina giving guidance and overseeing everything.

"The rolled sardines for the starter are ready," she announced to Davide with a grin of satisfaction.

Davide told her what had happened.

"Oh, no. We'll have to keep everyone indoors with all the shutters closed," she said with a sigh.

"We can't do that with this number of guests. I have another idea. But we must be very careful."

Davide explained his plan to Mamma, who thoroughly approved of it. She communicated it to the hired staff and, a little later, trays of food were ready to be loaded into cars. A beeline of staff carried food, drinks, cutlery and crockery from the kitchen's rear entrance to the cars parked just outside it.

Davide rolled the hog roast in an aluminium blanket and, with the help of another strong man, loaded it onto the roof of a four-wheel-drive, securing it with bungee ties.

Davide entrusted his car to one of the staff to drive down to the beach and said goodbye to Mamma.

"If I can leave here, I'll get on my bicycle and join you down at the beach. But I think I'll be too busy here."

"What about Eleonora?" Mamma Cristina asked.

"I need her here," he said stiffly.

This much was true, even if it wasn't the main reason he wanted her away from the action. But his mother wouldn't understand the other reason.

They staggered the cars' set off so that they wouldn't be as obvious as if they travelled in a convoy, should the paparazzo take his eyes off the lens and look down the road instead.

When the last car had departed, Davide closed the back door. The kitchen, which until a few minutes ago had been bustling with activity, was now quiet and empty.

The only people left in the trattoria were him,

Eleonora and the sleeping girls, but they would have to make as much noise as a whole party.

Davide went out onto the terrace.

"I've turned on the braziers, opened the umbrellas and put up the decorations. I can't lay the tables without going back inside," Eleonora said.

"Thanks, I'll stay out here until you come back."

Just as the paparazzo was keeping his tele lens on them, they needed to keep an eye on him to make sure he didn't move from where they wanted him—which was right there.

Eleonora returned quickly with a bewildered expression.

"Where is everyone? Where have all the wedding cutlery and crockery gone?"

"We'll have to use our normal cutlery and crockery for this, but it's okay. It won't look any different from a distance."

"I'm totally confused. What's going on?"

"Paolo and Alice's wedding party has moved but you and I will stay here to entertain the paparazzo."

Davide studied her reaction. If she were in cahoots with the paparazzo, this news would disappoint her. But there was no disappointment or irritation on her face. Only confusion.

"How?"

"By pretending the wedding is still happening here."

Eleonora's eyes widened.

"You and I are going to fake an entire wedding party?"

"With the girls' help, if they don't mind."

Her bewildered expression turned into an amused smile.

"I'm sure they will be delighted to be asked to make as much noise as possible. This sounds like fun."

This wasn't the reaction of a paparazzo's accomplice, Davide thought with relief and a pang of guilt.

"We'll need disguises," she said with a hint of excitement, "and music."

Davide turned on the trattoria's stereo system to a volume it had never been turned to before.

The twins woke up and were more than happy to do their part, frolicking and running around enough for a whole party of kids.

Eleonora closed some of the restaurant's shutters to give the party an aura of secrecy that fitted well with a celebrity's wedding. This would also make it easier for them to pretend there was a big number of people inside the restaurant by passing frequently in front of the few open windows wearing different clothes.

Davide and Eleonora brought an array of clothes downstairs and the game began.

The twins were electrified with excitement. It was a wacky cross between a fashion show and a magician's number, which involved walking in front of the window on bent knees to fake different heights, stuffing clothes with cushions to mimic different body shapes and putting on different voices. Sometimes they walked out onto the terrace to give the illusion of even more people.

Every now and then, Davide rushed upstairs and looked out of the window to make sure the paparazzo's scooter was still parked behind the bush down the road and the tele lens was still pointed at the same windows, the ones where Davide, Eleonora and the girls were doing their shows.

Meanwhile, Mamma Cristina sent them updates from the beach. The beaming bride and groom had arrived with their guests and they seemed very pleased with their wedding party in the unusual location. No paparazzi had turned up to spoil the fun and most of the villagers were too distracted with their own festive celebrations to have noticed the celebrity party at the beach.

Those who had realised what was going on, had volunteered to stand guard and chase away paparazzi and anyone with a camera or phone in their hands.

Davide was relieved that his plan was working well. If he, Eleonora and the girls could keep the paparazzo at the trattoria until the real wedding was over, it would all be alright.

Chapter 28

Eleonora

"You must pretend that you are the bride and the groom," Violetta told Eleonora and Davide.

"That's not necessary, sweetie," Eleonora said briskly.

"Yes, it is," Veronica joined in, supporting her sister.

Eleonora was usually pleased by the girls' loyalty to each other, but not on this occasion.

"Girls, it's your turn to go out onto the terrace," Davide said, deftly changing the topic.

"We won't do our work until you and Mummy do yours," Violetta said, folding her arms.

Oh, no. This was proper mutiny.

"We don't have the right clothes to dress up as the bride and the groom," Eleonora pointed out.

"You've got a white dress that you wear in the summer and a white scarf that you can put on your head."

The girls were right. Her white silk scarf would make a perfect bride's veil and her white dress could surely pass for a fashionably demure wedding dress from a distance. But being Davide's bride would be too much of a déjà vu.

"The girls are right. It would help if we dressed up as Paolo and Alice," Davide said, to her surprise.

"I don't look anything like Alice."

"You don't have to show your face. Just the back of a woman in a white veil will do."

"And you have to dress up as the groom and kiss her," Violetta said.

"Oh, no. No. That's not necessary," Davide said quickly.

Eleonora didn't like that at all. Why should she play her part while he was exonerated?

"Oh yes, it is. Very necessary," she contradicted him.

As surprise marbled his face, Eleonora realised her mistake. She hadn't just pressed for him to dress up but also for him to kiss her.

"I meant, if I must dress up, so must you," she quickly clarified.

But it was too late. The girls were already chanting, "Bride and groom! Kiss, kiss!"

"Just dressing up!" Eleonora protested in vain.

The girls weren't listening.

"The girls are right. We must play our part too," Davide said with a smile kicking up the corner on his mouth in challenge.

"Fine, then. Let's," Eleonora replied defiantly.

If he could kiss her, so could she. What was a kiss but a temporary touching of lips? They had kissed many times before, and one more certainly wouldn't rock her world.

Eleonora and Davide rushed upstairs to dress up while the girls continued to entertain the paparazzo through the windows.

Eleonora slipped into her white summer dress and spread her transparent white silk scarf on her head like a veil. She glanced at herself in the mirror. She looked more like a bride now than when she had actually been one. Back then, money was tight and she had worn a pink flowery dress that a friend had lent her because she didn't own any smart dresses.

She stepped out of her bedroom and her breath caught. Davide was just coming out of his room, wearing the suit he had worn at their wedding. He had kept it.

Memories flooded back, together with the same butterfly-in-the-stomach feeling she had felt on that day. Tanned, broader, rugged and head-shaven, he looked even more handsome now than he had back then. And her stupid legs wobbled a bit. She shouldn't feel this way.

Something soft and vulnerable passed through a chink in his impassive expression, but he quickly recovered himself.

"Ready?" he asked.

Was he suggesting they walked down the stairs together, arm in arm, like a real couple? No, that would surely be too much.

"After you," she said diplomatically.

Downstairs, the stereo system was blasting a romantic ballad. The girls must have changed the song. As they saw Eleonora and Davide appear, they began chanting "kiss, kiss!" to the ballad's tempo.

Davide picked a poinsettia flower from a table arrangement and put it in his lapel, then took another one and delicately threaded it through the strap of Eleonora's dress.

Even though he had avoided brushing her skin, a frisson ran over her, giving her goosebumps. Or maybe it was just his presence so close to her. How could he still have such an effect on her?

"Let's go to a window," he said.

She nodded, quickly reminding herself what this was all about—a performance for the paparazzo.

Davide positioned himself in front of the nearest window, facing inside so that his face would be hidden from the paparazzo. Eleonora joined him. His broad shoulders hid her completely. She took a tiny step to the side so that the paparazzo could see at least a sliver of bride.

Davide put a hand on her waist. A tingle of electricity ran up Eleonora's side. It felt shockingly natural and right for him to hold her like that, like two pieces of a puzzle coming together.

"Kiss, kiss!" the girls chanted, grinning.

Davide pulled her a little closer.

She was starting to regret agreeing to this. If just that closeness was enough to make her feel like prosecco was running through her veins, what would a kiss to do to her?

She looked up and met his gaze. And she immediately knew that she was not going to come out of this unscathed.

He lowered his face and their lips met. The feel of his lips, the scent of his skin—it was like coming home. She could no longer hear the girls' excited squeals or the music blaring. All she could hear was the frantic beating of her own heart, yearning for more.

He pulled away first.

Eleonora couldn't look into his eyes. Maybe she would never be able to look into his eyes again.

Had he felt the same as she had felt? Or maybe for him it had been nothing. Could he tell that she had felt something? Did he pity her for it?

She had no answer to all these questions, but one thing she knew for sure: there was still something between them, she could feel it as powerfully as her own heart.

But what good was it? They'd had their chance and it hadn't worked out. There had been disappointments, recriminations and shattered hearts. She didn't want to live through it ever again.

"Dance, dance!" Violetta and Veronica chanted.

"Greedy girls, we've done enough," Eleonora said, surprised at the catch in her voice.

"We've got dressed for the part, we might as well," Davide said.

His voice had changed too—a little rougher, a little deeper.

Eleonora made the mistake of looking at him. There was a tenderness in his eyes that she remembered from eons ago, from when he used to look at her as if she were the most precious thing in the world. A tenderness that said, "I've chosen you", and "You complete me".

Davide took her hand into his and she let him. The music was mellow and slow now, and she leaned against his shoulder. The scent of him inebriated her. She melted against him. They fitted together perfectly. She wished time could stand still and all her life could be made of moments like this.

Why should it still feel so good when it was all over between them?

This was wrong. They had accused each other of terrible things. There had been yelling, threats, insults and smashed plates. She couldn't go through that again.

"You're not in the window anymore," the girls told them.

They had got distracted and drifted away. They both quickly let go of each other and stepped away, suddenly realising what they had done. What dangerous feelings they had let take over.

"Right, enough of this. Everyone back to work," Eleonora said with two claps of her hands. She was urging herself more than anyone else.

She turned to go upstairs and get changed. But someone stood by the kitchen doors.

Chapter 29

Davide

"What kind of trick is this?" the man at the door snarled.

Davide recognised him immediately. He was the paparazzo.

Eleonora scowled at him.

"What are you doing here?"

"Where's the wedding?" the man rudely demanded to know.

"Who told you there was a wedding?"

"Not everyone in Altavicia is as stupidly loyal as you," the man said with a snort.

If Davide had needed any more proof of Eleonora's innocence, this had to be the conclusive one.

"Perhaps if Paolo and Alice had paid more for their wedding favours, the supplier might have been less forthcoming with me," the paparazzo added.

When Paolo had chosen a wedding favour

supplier from outside Altavicia, Davide had warned him against it. Altavicians would be loyal to their local celebrity tenor and wouldn't give his daughter away to the paparazzi, but someone from outside town might not be as devoted. Unfortunately, Altavicia's small gift shop didn't normally sell wedding favours. They would have ordered some in especially for Paolo and Alice, but Paolo had preferred to go with a supplier who specialised in it and could offer a wide choice. Sadly, this other supplier must have sold them out to the press.

"Why are you so desperate to ruin Paolo and Alice's day? Is it just for money?" Eleonora asked the man.

"It's easy to look down on money when you're not crushed by debt like I am. 'Just' money is why my wife and my children had to go live with the mother-in-law and why I'm alone this Christmas. But with the money from this scoop I'll be able to pay off the loan sharks and get my family back. So, where are the bride and the groom?"

"It's us," Davide said.

"You've already been married and divorced," the paparazzo said with a dismissive wave of his hand.

"How do you know that?"

"In our profession we're used to digging up people's pasts."

"So that they can blackmail people," Eleonora added.

So that coward hadn't just offered Eleonora

money but he had blackmailed her too, Davide realised. And despite it all, Eleonora still hadn't buckled. This must be why she had told Mamma Cristina about their marriage—so that Mamma could learn it from her rather than from the man.

"I also know all about your children," he said to Davide.

Davide's mind reeled. So it was true. He turned to Eleonora and her guilty expression confirmed it. Had everyone known that the girls were his daughters except for him?

The man smirked. "Oops, you didn't know yet," he said sarcastically.

"What's he saying?" Violetta asked stepping forward.

The man looked at Davide with crazed eyes. "Is it fair that people who don't even know they have children can spend Christmas with them while I can't spend Christmas with my family? I say it's not. So I'll take your children instead!"

He grabbed Violetta by the shoulder. She screamed. Davide flung himself at the man and lifted him by the collar.

"Let her go or I'll call the police. Everything you've done has been recorded by our CCTV," Davide growled at him. He was bluffing about the CCTV.

Suddenly, the man crumpled to the floor.

Violetta pulled away and ran into Eleonora's arms. The paparazzo covered his face with his hands and dissolved into sobs. "I'm s-sorry," he choked. "I don't know what came over me."

For a moment, they all watched him in stunned silence. Finally, Eleonora pushed a chair towards him and turned to the kitchen to get him a glass of water. Her eyes met Davide's as she passed, and he marvelled at the sympathy that filled them.

"You know," he said to the man, "There's a new law to help people overcome by debt. I can get you in touch with the offices that can help you."

The man looked at Davide with eyes filled with gratitude. "Thank you for your forgiveness."

The wedding was still going on at the beach and Mamma Cristina sent some of the staff to collect braziers and garden lights to carry on into the evening and, perhaps, even the night. The staff reported that the wedding was going very well, and some people had even gone swimming. Davide had no doubts who those people might be.

He agreed with Eleonora not to tell anyone about the paparazzo's attack quite yet, to avoid creating anxiety and spoiling the fun.

By now the news of Paolo and Alice's wedding party at the beach had done the round of the village, and many people had turned up with homemade dishes and folding tables to join in. The party had turned into a whole village event, with the famous Luigi Felice rubbing shoulders with the baker, the cobbler, the fisherman next door. Any one of them could have called the press or snapped photos to sell for money. But nobody had. No Altavician would give away their beloved celebrity tenor and his family.

The girls quickly recovered from the scary encounter with the paparazzo. Davide and Eleonora had turned off the blaring music, removed all the wedding props and tidied the restaurant.

Davide felt too emotionally exhausted to join the wedding party at the beach, and he urgently needed to talk to Eleonora. But without the girls.

Eleonora must have felt the same because she suggested an early supper and early bedtime for the girls.

Together, Davide and Eleonora whipped up a quick pasta soup—warming and comforting—cooking together like in the old times.

Then they sat down to supper, just the four of them, and it felt like they were a family. A knot formed in Davide's throat. This was what could have been.

"What was the man saying about Veronica and me?" Violetta asked after a few mouthfuls of soup.

Davide glanced at Eleonora but she averted her gaze.

"Nothing important."

"I heard him say 'your children'," Veronica said to Davide.

Eleonora squirmed on her chair, further

confirming that what everyone said about the girls was true. But clearly the girls' paternity wasn't a topic she wanted to broach in the girls' presence.

"If you're ready for bed in good time, I'll give you my Christmas pressie," Davide said to the girls.

"You have presents for them?" Eleonora asked, surprised.

"Yes."

He had bought them Christmas presents when he still hadn't even suspected that they might be his daughters. He had taken to these girls from the moment they had stood on the threshold of the office, leaning in but keeping their shoes behind the threshold.

"We'll be super quick!" the girls announced.

Chapter 30

Eleonora

While the girls were getting ready for bed and Davide was sweeping the restaurant, Eleonora washed up the supper dishes, relieved to be alone with her thoughts.

Davide hadn't looked very surprised when the paparazzo dropped the bombshell about the girls' paternity. Had he already guessed the truth? She must talk to him as soon as she'd tucked the girls into bed and before Mamma Cristina and the others came back.

"We're ready for bed! Can we have our pressies now?" the girls' excited voices drifted in from the restaurant.

"First, we need to check with your mum," Davide replied to them, then louder, "Ele, can I give them their presents now?"

Eleonora froze. Davide hadn't called her "Ele" since their relationship had started to unravel.

Why was he using her pet name now? Hearing him call her that made her chest glow with a warmth she hadn't felt for years.

The girls rushed into the kitchen in their pyjamas and slippers, grinning to show her their freshly brushed teeth.

"Good job," she told them, her voice trembling a little. Then to Davide, "Yes, you can!"

The girls ran back to him, leaving Eleonora in the kitchen.

She decided to stay there and give Davide this time alone with his daughters, especially now that he knew the truth.

As she tidied plates away and wiped worktops, she could hear squeals of delights from the other room and smiled to herself. It was so nice for the girls to have Davide in their lives, even if they didn't know that he was their dad, and he hadn't known it until a few hours ago.

She should have told him the truth earlier. Instead, by keeping quiet, she had deprived all three of a precious relationship. And what for? All because of her pride and fears.

The girls ran into the kitchen.

"Look, Mummy! We've got sailing boats!"

They thrusted two wooden sailing boat models into her hands. They were beautifully lacquered, one red and one blue. The sails were hand-stitched, with metal hoops and reinforcing patches, battens and even see-through windows for the sailor to see what was on the other side of the sail.

Davide walked in behind the girls and looked at her gingerly, as if her reaction mattered.

"Davide, they're beautiful. They must have cost a fortune," she blurted.

"I only had to pay for the materials."

He touched the back of his head in a shy, boyish way.

"You made them?"

He nodded.

These boats were not a token gesture from someone who felt a duty to produce a present for the children of the house. These boats were a labour of love.

For the next few minutes, Eleonora repeated to the girls that they must look after their boats, that they were not toys and they must never put them in the water. At the same time, Davide told the girls that they could absolutely put their boats in the water, that the boats were toys and they didn't need any looking after.

Eventually, Eleonora and Davide agreed to disagree and that it was time the girls went to bed.

"But we want to play with the boats!" the twins protested.

"You can play with them in your beds so long as you don't get out of bed or leave your room," Eleonora decreed.

The girls hugged Davide and kissed him goodnight, which gave Eleonora a slight knot in her throat. Then she accompanied them upstairs, said their bedtime prayers with them, and wished them goodnight.

She closed the door and was about to go back downstairs to find Davide but he had come up with two glasses of wine.

"Drink?" he asked.

"Yes, please."

She was certainly going to need it.

They sat on Mamma Cristina's sofa, in front of the window that looked out to the sea. A glow from the direction of the beach told them that the party was still going, under the cheerful rhythmic sweep of the lighthouse's beam.

They sat in silence for a while, looking out of the window.

"It's true, isn't it?" he asked.

"Yes."

"Why didn't you tell me?"

"At first it was pride. You had won the battle over children and I had lost it."

"It wasn't a battle."

"I know, but it felt like it. Also, I was afraid that, if you knew about the pregnancy, you would backtrack on the divorce and try to persuade me to stay with you."

He hesitated.

"And would that have been such a terrible thing?" he said gingerly.

Eleonora wasn't expecting him to say this. Did he regret their divorce? Did she?

No, these questions were too big to deal with

right now. She went on.

"I'm just telling you how I felt back then. By the time I decided that I was overreacting and that you and the girls deserved to know each other, too much time had passed and you had gone to sea. How could I tell you that you had two daughters out of the blue?"

"So you decided instead that you were never going to tell me."

"I didn't decide anything. I just put off the decision. Maybe, subconsciously, coming to work for your mum was a way to get closer to you and eventually tell you. I don't know. But I know that I still didn't feel ready when you suddenly came back."

He nodded.

"At least, now your coming here makes sense."

She exhaled with relief.

"Finally. All your suspicions about my motives were quite hurtful. I admit that it was a stupid plan, but I was in a panic."

"I'm sorry. If you had let me know, I would have helped."

"You couldn't have. I needed someone to teach me how to be a good mother. I didn't want to be a distant mother like mine. If I didn't have bad-mother genes in me, I surely had no good example to copy so I was sure to be a bad mother too."

"Was this why you hadn't wanted children?"

"I guess so."

"If you had told me, everything would have

made more sense. We could have worked through it." he said.

"I didn't realise it myself." She took a deep breath. "So there I was, on my own, feeling that I was failing to be a good mother. In desperation, I turned to the one person I knew for sure had been a good mother—yours. From the way you had talked about your childhood, I knew that she was the example I needed. So I came here to give the girls a grandma and to give myself a role model."

Another thought came to her, so clear that she was shocked she had never realised it before. She had come to Mamma Cristina to be near that piece of Davide she had never been part of.

"What are your plans now? Are you going to tell the girls that I'm their father? How about Mamma? Anyone else?" he asked.

"Only if you want to."

"I want to be in the girls' life. I want to be their dad." His voice caught. "I've missed out on seeing them being born and grow into what they are now. I will never get that back—"

"I'm sorry," she interrupted.

"—but I will not miss a moment more. I can't deny that I'm cross with you for keeping this secret from me, but I will always be thankful that you kept the girls, gave birth to them and brought them up. You didn't want children and could have easily chosen not to keep them, but you didn't. Thank you."

A knot formed in Eleonora's throat. She felt so

guilty for keeping the secret that she certainly hadn't expected to be thanked.

"And if I ever forget what you've done, any time in the future, feel free to remind me."

He had said "any time in the future". He saw a future for them.

"Thank you," she said. "Tomorrow we should tell the girls and your mum. Then rest of the town will easily get to know, I'm sure."

Chapter 31

Davide

When Eleonora and Davide broke the news, the girls squealed with happiness. Mamma's reaction wasn't much different. Much to her delight, the girls started to call her "Nonna", and she showered them with hugs and kisses.

As Davide and Eleonora had anticipated, the news travelled quickly through Altavicia and became intertwined with that of the paparazzo's attack and Davide's daring intervention.

Unfortunately, Mamma now had more ammunition than ever to push for Davide and Eleonora's reunion.

"Make Eleonora an honest woman and marry her again," Mamma pleaded with Davide when Eleonora and the girls were out.

"The girls were conceived when Eleonora and I were still married so, technically, Eleonora has always been an 'honest' woman."

"But why not get married again? It's obvious that you still love each other, it's clear," Mamma insisted.

In truth, Davide couldn't forget what Eleonora had said—that she hadn't told him about the girls for fear that he would refuse her a divorce. Even when she knew that she was expecting his child, she hadn't stopped wanting a divorce. Then why should she want to get back together now? He hadn't done anything that would make her change her mind. Since he had arrived, he had done nothing but mistrust her and accuse her of horrible things.

Of course he couldn't tell Mamma this or she would turn her reunion campaign on Eleonora, and she didn't deserve to be put under that pressure.

"Please, drop this subject and let Eleonora and I live our own lives—in privacy."

He kissed her twice on the cheeks and went to the door. Today he was going to meet Paolo at Camillo's Café.

He still hadn't had a chance to give his best friend the news about the twins, and Paolo must have already heard it through the grapevine. Davide needed to put things right and tell him himself.

It was raining hard so Davide ran from the trattoria to the car and dived in. That short distance had been enough to soak him and the windscreen immediately steamed up.

Davide's gaze fell on the rental company's sticker. Yes, this wasn't his car and Altavicia wasn't his home. He was only here on borrowed time. Soon he would return the car to the airport's rental desk and get onto an aeroplane to wherever the yacht had reached during these last few weeks.

Capitano Armorio had been very understanding and had told him to take as much time as he needed, but now that Mamma was back on her feet and Christmas was over, Davide couldn't justify staying any longer.

He smiled wryly to himself, remembering how, only a few weeks ago, he had been desperate to leave Altavicia. How relieved he had been to hear that the job on the yacht was still waiting for him.

Now he wished Capitano Armorio had dismissed him and he didn't have to leave his daughters so soon after meeting them. And Eleonora.

He couldn't deny that the old feelings were still there. When they had played bride and groom, kissing her had felt as right as breathing. Like coming home.

He looked at the trattoria's building. It was big enough, he could easily live with them without being in Eleonora's way. Each had their own rooms and they had already proven that they could successfully avoid each other if they wanted to. During the busy periods there would be enough work for him too, and during the quiet ones he could find casual cheffing work in Reggio Calabria.

It would be sad for him to leave Capitano Armorio and the rest of the crew, but they'd surely find someone to replace him. Yes, he could give up his job and stay.

Just then, the van of *The Scarlet Pimpernel*, Altavicia's florist, pulled into the carpark.

As far as Davide knew, there was no special event in the trattoria that day or in the coming days, and they still had all the Christmas greenery and plants from Paolo and Alice's wedding. What could the van possibly be doing here today?

The passenger door opened and Eleonora jumped out and ran into the trattoria with a flower bouquet in her hands. Then the van turned around and drove off.

Davide suddenly felt his throat turn to cardboard.

All this time he had worried about the girls' father—without knowing that that man was him —and hadn't thought that Eleonora could still have a relationship with any other man.

Giovanni sold flowers and books. What could be more romantic? And he was a thoroughly good guy. No wonder Eleonora had fallen for him.

Davide pushed away the sadness that was creeping into his heart. He had no right to be sad. He had asked to be in the girls' lives and he had been granted that. He had not asked to be in Eleonora's life. For that, he had had his chance and had rejected it.

There was no point in getting nostalgic and

maudlin about the past. He must look to the future. He had two lovely daughters he was falling in love with more every day. He would find a way to be a good father to them without encroaching on Eleonora's life and her future with another man, whoever that might be.

No, staying back at Mamma's trattoria was out of the question. Eleonora needed her space without an ex-husband always hovering in the background, sharing the same flat.

Altavicia was too small a place. Everyone in Altavicia knew him and, now, they also knew his history with her. It wouldn't be right for him to stay.

He must call Capitano Armorio today and tell him that he was ready to return to his job.

He turned on the engine and drove off.

Chapter 32

Eleonora

Eleonora stepped into the trattoria and shook the rain off her coat. Just dashing from Giovanni's van to the trattoria's door had been enough to soak her. She dreaded to think how wet she would have got if Giovanni hadn't offered her a lift.

He was a lovely man, and today he had asked her if her relationship with Davide was completely over.

Since they'd broken the news of their past marriage and of the girls' parentage, Eleonora and Davide had been the talk of the town, but not maliciously. Most people were rooting for them to get back together, but Giovanni was very obviously not one of them—he had made no mystery of his wish to marry Eleonora.

It would be so easy to love him back, but Eleonora couldn't. There was no point in hiding it from herself anymore: she was—back? still?—in love with Davide.

She had suspected it the moment he had walked back into the trattoria, she had denied it every day since, but she had it confirmed when he had kissed her in front of the window. Then, watching him save Violetta from the deranged paparazzo had lodged him firmly into her heart.

So when Giovanni asked her if it was all over between her and Davide, Eleonora had answered yes but hadn't made any effort to hide her disappointment.

She and Davide would never get back together, but she still loved him anyway.

She put the bouquet down on the ottoman and shrugged off her coat. Then she picked up the beautiful bouquet again and walked into the kitchen.

Mamma Cristina was preparing her wonderful sauces—three of them at once, because Mamma's cooking was the full symphony.

Eleonora greeted her and Mamma Cristina turned. She saw the bouquet in Eleonora's hands and grinned.

"You've received some flowers!"

"No, this is for you," Eleonora said, handing her the bouquet.

The smiled drained from Mamma's face.

"It's from Giovanni, the florist. He says these are not 'get well' flowers but 'got well' ones. He's very happy to hear that you're well again and he sends you his good wishes."

"That's very sweet of him," Mamma said without enthusiasm.

"What's wrong, Mamma?"

"I thought these flowers were for you from Davide." She sighed. "When will my boy get his act together and start trying to woo you back?"

Eleonora felt a small lump in the back of her throat but she wasn't sure if she was feeling sorry for Mamma or for herself.

"There's no point in trying to woo me. We've had our chance," she said.

"Why only one? Life is full of second chances. My son of all people should know."

"Why?"

"Has he never told you about his father?"

"All I know is that he died."

"That was his stepfather. His biological father abandoned me when I got pregnant with Davide. This is why I moved to Altavicia. This town isn't where I originally come from. That's why we have only my husband's family here, not mine. I wanted to escape the gossip, the disapproving glances and the pitying looks, so I came here to start from scratch. I worked in this trattoria, which was called *Mamma Rosa's Trattoria*, and Mamma Rosa took me under her wing and looked after me and my son. A lovely Altavician man, Pietro, fell in love with me and I with him, and we got married. Mamma Rosa welcomed him too at the trattoria. Every morning, Pietro drove down to the town to his mechanic's shop, then he would come back every evening and help serve dinner if we were busy or play with Davide or fix things around the trattoria. Unfortunately, he died a few years later. Then Mamma Rosa died and she left the trattoria to me and Davide."

"So that's why you welcomed me and gave me a roof—because you had been a single mum like me."

"You could say that. Or you could say that I liked you and your girls as soon as I met you."

Eleonora thought about all this. How little she and Davide had known each other. Their marriage had been so brief and shallow that she hadn't known even the most basic information about his family. Had they really given their relationship a proper chance, or had the issue of children blinded them to everything else about each other?

"I wish you and Davide would get back together, but I'm sure you've already guessed that."

"Davide must go back to the yacht," Eleonora said.

"Well, yes, and that's inconvenient, but many people have spouses at sea and they somehow make it work. When Pietro and I got together, we had some difficult choices to make, despite us both living in Altavicia. He thought he would lose his customers if he didn't live above his shop anymore, and I didn't want to leave the trattoria. In the end, he moved here and discovered that customers still came to his shop. The only difference was that they now had to respect his opening times and couldn't call on him at all hours of the day and night."

Mamma gazed into the distance and smiled, lost in her memories.

That was what Davide would be for her—bad memories forgotten and sweet memories put away in the storerooms of her mind. That kiss by the window when they were playing bride and groom, would go in with the other memories too, and that would be all.

Chapter 33

Davide

A hopeful wintery sun had come out of the clouds and cast a rainbow over the few patches of rain still lingering over the mountains.

Davide drove up to the trattoria after his meeting with Paolo. His friend was going on honeymoon and then straight to London, so this had been Davide and Paolo's goodbye.

Davide had told his friend about seeing Eleonora with Giovanni and about his consequent decision to leave Altavicia and give her space. What he hadn't told Paolo was that seeing Eleonora with another man was too painful, and staying in Altavicia would inevitably mean more of this.

Paolo had urged him to talk to Eleonora and leave no misunderstandings between them. They must discuss everything from how much she expected— or tolerated—him to be part of the girls' lives, to how much money he should contribute to the girls' upbringing, to what the girls should call him and a possible future stepdad. It was going to be a painful conversation but a necessary one, and they needed to have it immediately.

Chapter 34

Eleonora

Eleonora had gone out to the garden to collect some rosemary and bay leaves for the kitchen but she had been caught by the view.

The sea was a patchwork of grey, ultramarine, cobalt and turquoise, with beams of sunlight piercing through indigo clouds and sparkling on the waves. The patches of turquoise reminded her of the colour of Davide's eyes.

And there he was, pulling into the car park just as she was thinking about him. It wasn't a big coincidence, given that she thought of him quite a lot.

She waved at him but he didn't wave back. Instead, he stepped out of the car and started walking towards her with a serious, concerned expression. Something must be wrong. She put her herb basket down on the rocks.

"Ele, we need to talk."

That pet name again. A frisson of pleasure ran up her back.

"Sure. Now?"

"Anytime before I go."

"Aren't you staying for lunch?"

"I meant, before I leave Altavicia."

That felt like a rock landing on her stomach. All these days she had been trying not to think about his return to the yacht.

"When are you leaving?"

"Tomorrow evening."

Now the rock felt like an avalanche. How could he be leaving so soon? In all these weeks, he had never talked about his job and she had almost forgotten that Mamma's trattoria wasn't it.

"Can we talk now?" he asked.

There was still time before they had to open the restaurant for lunch, and Mamma Cristina had everything under control in the kitchen.

"Sure."

She gestured to the bench and they sat down.

"What is it about?"

"I want to discuss arrangements about the girls."

Eleonora felt a prick of disappointment. So it wasn't about them.

"I want to be present in their lives."

His tone was firm and his jaw set, ready to fight if Eleonora disagreed.

It saddened her that he thought she might oppose his wish, but she couldn't blame him for it:

173

she had kept the girls' existence a secret from him for five years.

"Of course."

"I would like them to call me 'dad' but if this is reserved for their stepdad—"

"Stepdad?"

"When you marry your new man and start a new family, if their stepdad will want to be called 'dad', I will understand."

"I'm not planning on marrying again."

"It's okay, Ele, you can do it. I will completely understand if you want to start a new relationship with someone else."

Why was he talking about new relationships? Was he trying to squash any hopes she might have of getting back together? Or perhaps he was giving her his blessing because he wanted hers back. Maybe he had met someone on the yacht and was preparing to break the news. Now that they were coparenting, she would eventually find out if he had a new partner in any case.

"Thank you, and the same applies to you. You are completely free to start a new relationship," she said, trying to sound breezy and nonchalant.

"Of course, I will send you my contribution to the girls' maintenance, regardless of whether you're on your own or with someone else," he added.

Her chest squeezed. He was paying her off. Maybe he had someone else and, when he had told her that he had two daughters, she had reacted negatively. So he was paying his way out of this unforeseen complication.

"There's no need. Your mother has given me a job."

"I want to contribute."

"I'd rather you didn't."

He looked hurt.

"Okay. I understand."

She doubted he did but she wasn't going to contradict him. This conversation was getting too painful and she wanted it to be over.

She picked up her basket.

"Can you please break the news of your departure to the girls? I'd rather not be the one to do it."

"Of course."

"Goodbye, then, Davide."

"Goodbye, Ele."

He looked unsure, then awkwardly hugged her and kissed her on the cheek. It was a brotherly kiss, so different from the one they had exchanged by the window that she wished he had just walked away instead.

Chapter 35

Eleonora

I t was the feast of the Epiphany, the last of the Christmas season's celebrations. Tomorrow the schools would open again and the holiday period would be over.

Eleonora looked forward to normality. She was under no illusion that her life would be back to how it was before Davide's visit, but at least she could pretend.

Davide had been gone for three days and, by tacit agreement, Eleonora and Mamma had avoided talking about him, each nursing her nostalgia on her own.

The girls had been sad for the first day but then had been distracted by the preparations for returning to school.

Eleonora had coped by throwing herself into her work—which was a very good thing because today the trattoria was busy.

Every table was taken by families celebrating

the festivity of the three kings, and the restaurant was buzzing with children excited about the pressies and sweets the Befana had brought to them on this day.

Violetta and Veronica, too, were excited, and had eaten too many sweets.

Eleonora was writing down an order of *bruschette* and 'nduja when Violetta ran into her and hugged her waist from behind.

The rule was that, when the trattoria was open and Eleonora was serving, the girls weren't allowed to disturb her unless there was an emergency.

"What are you doing?" she asked sharply.

"He's back!" Violetta replied.

"Who's back?"

"Daddy!"

Eleonora stilled. There was only one man the girls could call with that name, but he couldn't be there. He was sailing on some faraway ocean, in another kitchen, cooking for other people.

"He can't be," Eleonora said, but then she looked up.

There was Davide, as rugged and handsome as when he had walked through that door a few weeks ago, taking her breath away like he was doing now.

That time he had looked at her with shock and suspicion. This time, his eyes showed a new softness and vulnerability.

Eleonora forgot about the family whose orders

she was taking, the couple who had asked for the bill and the woman who had asked for another bottle of water. Nothing around her existed anymore but this man who was walking towards her with the air of someone who had something important to say.

The happiness at seeing him again suddenly turned to worry. Why wasn't he on the yacht? Had he been fired? Had he had an accident?

"Is everything okay?" she asked.

"I hope so."

"What happened to your job?"

"I've turned it down."

Her chest felt as if someone had filled it with helium. If Davide had turned down the job, he couldn't have a woman on the yacht.

"I want to stay in Altavicia. I want to see my daughters grow up," he continued.

"That's good."

"There's something else."

By now, the whole restaurant had fallen silent and everyone was looking at them. Eleonora barely registered it. Hope was blossoming in her heart even if she tried to squash it.

"I didn't tell you before I left because I wanted to give you space. But when I was out there at sea, I thought long and hard and decided that you must know. You can do with this information whatever you want, and you can be reassured that I will never mention it again after today. But you must know."

"Know what?" Eleonora asked faintly, her breath catching in her throat.

"I'm still in love with you, Ele."

Eleonora dropped her notepad on the floor.

"You can go with Giovanni and forget what I've just said. I will stay out of your way and rent a place for myself, but I want to stay here in Altavicia and see our daughters grow up—whether you want to give our relationship another chance or not. But I really hope that you do, because I can't stop loving you. You can't imagine how hard I've tried."

Everyone in the restaurant was holding their breath. All Eleonora could hear was the fireworks exploding in her heart.

"I do, I want to give us another chance. Because, Davide, I love you too."

Davide scooped her into his arms and held her tight as tears pricked the back of her eyes. The restaurant exploded in applause and cheers.

Violetta and Veronica hugged their legs, binding them all together.

"Kiss! Kiss!" the girls shouted.

Eleonora and Davide easily, gladly, obliged.

The End

Books In This Series

The Calabrian Coast Series

The Italian Fake Date

When Alice Baker discovers that she's been adopted, she knows she won't have peace until she's found her Italian birth mother. But all she has is a letter written twenty-five years ago and an old address.

Jaded about love and unable to forgive his ex-fiancée and his brother, Paolo Rondino is struggling to find inspiration for a sculpture that will make or break his career. Hoping that a trip home will help him find his muse again, he decides to return to Italy, even if this means confronting the two people who betrayed him.

Alice and Paolo strike a deal: he will help her find her birth mother and she will pretend to be his girlfriend to please his mother. It looks like the perfect exchange, until real feelings start to grow…

This novella is part of a series but is completely standalone.

Sweet Competition For Camillo's Café

Camillo runs a popular café on Altavicia's main square. Giada runs an equally popular café across the square. They have both entered Altavicia's Best Café competition.

Traumatised by his father's death, Camillo's greatest wish is to escape the Calabrian seaside village and return to his beloved London, where his family was last together and happy. Abandoned by her parents, Giada's greatest wish is to earn her nonna's love. The competition trophy is the ticket to both their dreams, but only one can win.

As Camillo discovers that happiness doesn't come from a location and Giada that love isn't earned, can enemies become friends, and maybe more?

This novella is part of a series but is completely standalone.

Books By This Author

How To Choose A Husband

Grazia Colonna has waited fifty years to meet The One. Now that her best friend is getting married for the second time, Grazia is sure that she'll meet The One at Rebecca's wedding. He will sweep Grazia off her feet and snatch her from the clutches of her bullying mother.

But first Grazia needs to alter the dress she will wear at the event and, for this, she needs the help of the village's grumpy widower tailor, Hector Gonzales.

As the bride is stuck abroad and may not get back in time for the wedding, Grazia and Hector are forced to work together and, inconveniently, they fall in love.

Can they ensure that the right wedding goes ahead and the wrong one doesn't?

Under Far Eastern Skies

Everyone thinks that thirty-one-year-old Shona Wells should get married: her overbearing father,

her starry-eyed little sister, and the whole expat community in 1930s Singapore. But Shona wants independence and the freedom to choose her own way, to travel the world exploring nature.

The last thing twenty-five-year old Will Palmer needs is marriage. He's too busy discovering new plant species in the remotest jungles in the world.

But then, three days before Shona is due to sail back to England, she meets Will, and finds someone with the same passion for the natural world. They are perfect for each other, until a series of misadventures and misunderstandings threatens to pull them apart forever.

Stars Are Silver

Is it too late for Melina to learn to drive? Is Don Pericle's vow never to fall in love again still valid after fifty years? Will a falling piano squash Filomena or just shake up her heart? Why does the mother of the bride ask Don Pericle to cancel the wedding?

Confetti And Lemon Blossom

For Don Pericle, wedding organising is a calling, not just a career. Deep in the Sicilian countryside, between rose gardens and trellised balconies, up marble staircases and across damasked ballrooms, these charming stories unfold: stories of star-crossed love, of comedic misunderstandings and of deep friendships, of love triumphing in the face of adversity. To these brides and grooms-to-be, Don Pericle becomes a guru, a mentor, even a friend, solving problems, untangling knots, rearranging menus and transforming lives. Fishmongers and Ferrari drivers, dressmakers and divorcees, gardeners and grandmothers: within the walls of Villa Lingualarga, all are offered a new chance at understanding each other – and maybe even finding true love.

Ten short stories perfect for your coffee break.

Fresh From The Sea

Will Gnà Peppina give her customers what they need, even if it's more than food? What pleasures can a man indulge in after his wife has put him on a draconian diet? Who will be able to cook dinner for the family with five euros?

A Season Of Goodwill

How far should Viviana's family go to avoid being thirteen at the table? Should Melina and Tanino attend a New Year's party hosted by Melina's old flame? Why do Don Pericle's clients want a Christmas wedding at all costs?

Ten humorous and heart-warming short stories shining with the Sicilian sunshine, fragrant with red wine and ringing with Christmas bells, perfect for the festive season.

What's Yours Is Mine

Can Melina give away her husband's possessions because they've always said that 'what's mine is yours and what's yours is mine'? Will the 'Sleep Doctor' deliver on his promises? How will the young Sicilian duke, Pericle, help his friend get married?

Five humorous and emotional short stories dripping with the Sicilian sunshine, ringing with street-sellers' singsongs, fragrant with freshly fried arancine rice balls.

Drive Me Crazy

"Cohabitation is tribulation" goes an Italian saying, and after more than fifty years of married life, Tanino and Melina know a thing or two about the challenges of living together.

Follow their antics as they compete to give their grandchild the best birthday present, struggle to lose some extra weight, and try to make it to their godchild's christening on time in this collection of twelve short stories dedicated entirely to the much-loved Sicilian couple from the pages of The People's Friend magazine.

Welcome To Quayside

Forty-year-old Tanya Baker dreams of starting a

new life and making friends when she moves to a block of flats by the River Thames with her thirteen-year-old daughter, Hattie.

But as Tanya and Hattie knock on neighbours' doors in search of a tin opener, it's clear that the residents of Number One Quayside like to keep to themselves. Everyone, that is, except their next-door neighbours, Italian chef Giacomo Dalamo, and his thirteen-year-old daughter, Frankie.

Between a delicious dish of lasagne (Giacomo's) and a burnt salad (Tanya's), they hatch a plan to set a library of things in their building, so that residents can borrow rarely-used items, from DIY tools to sports equipment and party supplies.

First, though, Tanya and Giacomo must win over their neighbours, persuade the building's management company, source library stock by kayaking down the Thames, and deal with plumbing disasters, all the while trying to protect their bruised hearts from falling for each other.

As all the residents at Quayside pull together to make the library happen, dreams are fulfilled, a community is born and love blossoms again.

Divided into thirty-one short self-contained chapters, this popular series from The People's Friend includes one brand-new story never published before.

Tales From The Parish

Father Okoli dreams of owning a flock of hens and

studying for a PhD, when his bishop saddles him with yet another parish to look after.

But as Father moves to Moreton-on-the-Edge, a farming village in the English Cotswolds, he's plugged into a community of warm-hearted characters, from the motherly parish secretary to her septuagenarian neighbour who's become a cycling champion, and from teenagers requiring driving lessons to atheist publicans who believe in miracles.

Between a wacky race and a scarecrow competition, a village fête and a mop fair, Father foils cattle rustlers, fends off foxes and goes viral on the internet. As the community pulls together to reopen the village's Electric Picture House, dreams are fulfilled, teen love blossoms and Father Okoli feels that Moreton-on-the-Edge is now home.

To Be Loved

Amanda's name means "to be loved" and she's taken it as her duty to make herself lovable, but it's hard work. Has Tanino really abandoned Melina to freeze at home? Mark hasn't seen Nora for thirty years and, since then, he's lost a leg and all his hair. If he wasn't enough for her then, how can he be now? What happens if the dating app's algorithms go haywire?

Sand, Sea And Tamburello

When Rosetta dries her hair on her balcony, she's not interested in the sun's warmth but in the young fishmonger who's eager to warm her heart. Can Don Pericle be a gracious host when an entire wedding party gets stranded at his villa? Tanino and Melina have a tough job competing with Valentina's other grandparents who take her on exhilarating trips to the beach. What can Alfonso do when his neighbours' karaoke parties become too much?

Ten stories that sparkle with the Sicilian sea, ring with the singsongs of fishmongers, and warm the heart like the summer's sun.

Father Roberto And The Missing Money

Two short cosy mysteries featuring a young Catholic priest in a Sicilian parish—perfect for fans of Father Brown, Sister Boniface and Don Matteo.

The Holiday Heist:
When young Sicilian Catholic priest Father Roberto finds an envelope full of cash lying on the floor by the church's nativity scene, he assumes it's a Christmas donation for his cash-strapped parish. But it turns out that the unexpected windfall isn't for keeping, and it lands the inexperienced priest

in a heap of trouble just at the parish's busiest time of year—the run-up to Christmas. Only by finding the real culprits can Father Roberto rid himself of the suspicion of robbery and get back to doing the job he loves.

The Missing Money:

In the seminary, nobody taught Father Roberto how to take a large group of children safely across a busy Palermo road. But as the young priest learns the ropes of being a children's summer camp leader for the parish, an unexpected problem emerges: the money put aside for the children's activities keeps disappearing.

Just as Roberto believes he's found the culprit, he discovers that the innocent are guilty and the guilty are innocent.

Keeping It Cool

Every good mum knows how to keep her daughter safe. But how will Izzy's mum cope on a visit to a perilous ice rink? Josh thinks Elise's boyfriend wish list is rather unusual. Can he tick all the boxes? Mario knows that his name is as common in Italy as John Smith. But why are his friends sending him funeral wreaths?

Ten humorous and uplifting stories, perfect for your coffee break.

Father Roberto And The Runaway Ring

The Runaway Ring

When well-to-do parishioner, Signora Albi, asks Father Roberto to recommend a trustworthy housekeeper, he puts forward Tano. The teenage boy knows how to keep house and he badly needs a job to keep himself out of trouble.

But when Signora Albi's precious engagement ring goes missing, she has no doubt that Tano is the culprit and that the young priest is his unwitting accomplice.

Now Roberto must find the missing ring before Signora Albi's deadline if he is to get himself and his young friend off the hook.

The Elopers' Escapade

There's nothing Father Roberto likes more than praying in the empty church at night, when nobody can interrupt him. But an eloping couple has other ideas. Seeking refuge from their rival criminal families, the star-crossed lovers demand that Roberto marries them then and there. Roberto would normally turn to his superior, Father Pietro, but he's mysteriously missing.

Can Roberto find Father Pietro and keep the Sicilian Romeo and Juliet safe from their families?

Two heartwarming cosy mysteries featuring a young priest in a Sicilian parish—perfect for fans of Chesterton's Father Brown, Jan Karon's Mitford series and the Grantchester mysteries

Father Roberto And The Rural Riots

Two heartwarming cosy mysteries featuring a young priest in a Sicilian parish—perfect for fans of Chesterton's Father Brown, Jan Karon's Mitford series and the Grantchester mysteries.

A Slip Of The Tongue

Will Melina regret faking to be sick to avoid her chores? Can Don Pericle organise a wedding for a groom who doesn't know? Who has stolen the marble pisces from the cathedral's floor?

Good Habits

Sister Luce loves her quiet life in the convent in the Italian Apennine mountains. In the company of her hens, among chestnut groves and fir forests, the shy young nun is at her happiest.

But Mother Speranza has invited a TV crew into their convent to shoot a documentary about their life, and she asks Sister Luce to be the convent's poster girl.

Never has Sister Luce's vow of obedience been so sorely tested, especially when four worldly women come to share the convent's life under the camera's lens.

Between a Santa dash and a carnival float, a forest sit-in and a song competition, Sister Luce becomes performer, protester, agony aunt and equestrian nun as she learns to conquer her fears.

Divided into thirty-one short self-contained small chapters, this popular series from The People's Friend magazine includes one brand-new story never published before.

About The Author

Stefania Hartley

Stefania Hartley was born in Sicily and immediately started growing, but not very much. She left her sunny island after falling head over heels in love with an Englishman, and now she lives in the UK with her husband and their three children.

Having finally learnt English, she's enjoying it so much that she now writes short stories and romance novels.

Subscribe to her newsletter to get first news of her latest releases and offers, and receive an exclusive free short story:

http://www.stefaniahartley.com/subscribe/

Praise For Author

Hartley doesn't just give us stories, she gives us a slice of Italian life served with lashings of charm and wit. Highly recommended!

- ELLA HAYES, AUTHOR OF ITALIAN SUMMER WITH THE SINGLE DAD

Hartley's stories are a tonic: full of delightful, down-to-earth characters and recognisable life dilemmas, as well as unexpected twists. Above all, each story reminds us that simple human goodness can still be found and shared.

- SANDY SALISBURY, AUTHOR OF PRAIRIE GOLD

www.ingramcontent.com/pod-product-compliance
Lightning Source LLC
Chambersburg PA
CBHW060437180626
46817CB00007B/2860